Perchero

By

Stephen Bill

ISBN: 9798541984637

www.publishnation.co.uk

Cover design by Scott Gaunt.

Original artwork: Rosa Bonheur, The Horse Fair, 1852-55.

For Larry, who kicked the whole thing off and travelled across the ocean with me.

ONE

Everything comes to an end. You sense it, you deny it, but there comes a point when you know it; it's the nature of all things.

Irwin knows it as he urges his gasping horse to go ever faster. The chase, he knows, is pointless. What he doesn't know is that a wire now stretches as far as the eye can see across the plain ahead. The wild horses see it first, swerving sharply, one stumbling, before they hurtle off in a new direction. Irwin sees it, calling out to his brother and the two riders pull their horses up short. 'Barbed wire… Well I'll be...' and as horse and rider fight for breath, Irwin knows that this is it. It feels as final as the finishing line at Saratoga.

They stare ahead, beyond the wire. In the far distance dust rises where a number of twenty horse hitches pull huge ploughs in formation, gouging their way across virgin land. It's hypnotising – the sheer scale of the spectacle. The younger of the two lads eventually turns to watch their quarry becoming ever smaller as they race away. 'Let'em go…' the older brother mutters as he looks down at the wire. With one hand he feels its tautness then removes his glove to feel the sharpness of the barb. His other hand relaxes its grip on the reins. The horse snorts his relief and lowers its head to the green shoots pushing up through old growth. Irwin sighs, 'It's over Jed.' The younger boy steadies his frothing horse, looks at his brother, follows his eyeline out beyond the fence towards the horizon. He can see the giant rigs, but doesn't understand, 'What is? What's over Irwin?'

He still doesn't understand as they make their way into a one-street town. Their failure has left him weary, his throat dust-dry, 'But Irwin, we promised Pa! We promised him twenty horses!'

'They've gone Jed, how many times…? The wild horses is finished, just like the buffalo.'

'Then we go to Montana, we go to Nebraska!'

They stop outside the dry goods store. As he ties up his horse Irwin scans the street. He watches a couple of linemen, still wearing their harnesses. They turn into the saloon. An old farmer rides slowly by in a rickety cart pulled by an ox. Irwin raises his hand to the man, but the glazed eyes see nothing. The two of them stand for a while, also saying nothing, exhausted by hours in the saddle. Irwin silently ticks off the things he's got to do – *go to the bank, buy supplies, buy dressmaking stuff for my sister*... There shouldn't be a problem, the town's not looking too bad, there's people about. Word used to be that the railroad passing through Abilene would kill it, but that seems not to be the case. He looks up and down the street one more time. 'Come on...' He starts to head for the saloon when someone calls his name. 'Irwin!'

'Mattie!'

A young woman comes running up the street. 'I've been waiting Irwin....'

'Things didn't go so good.' He takes some coins from his pocket and hands them to Jed. 'Get yourself a drink, but go easy now.'

Jed takes the money, smirks at his brother and backs away.

There are a number of men sitting at the bar with no easy clear space for him to stand. He feels suddenly conspicuous and filthy. Some of the men have suits, He'd been away from home for weeks, he guessed he didn't smell too good. There were those at the tables playing cards who looked more like his sort of folks, but he needed to get to the bar... He pulls his hat down and hopes the newly emerging moustache and hairy chin would make him look older than his fifteen years. A woman at one of the tables looks his way and smiles. He panics and moves.

On the street Irwin twists Mattie's hair between his fingers, she is searching his eyes. He looks away, she touches her hand to his cheek, making him look at her again. They kiss. 'This ain't no way to go on Irwin...'

'It's the way it is. I can't stay.'

'We still going West?'

'I figured Oklahoma.'

'When?'

'As soon as...'

'All those things you promised...'

'I know, I know.. but right now... I gotta go.'

He backs away, trying to explain about family, about responsibilities, how he desperately needs a drink, but she won't let him leave her. When they'd first met things were different. He had money in his pocket. Apart from those he'd paid for, she was his first girl, he'd thought of her every moment of every day, included her in his dreams, in the future they were going to share. He'd blurted out every single thing he felt. Everything had seemed possible. He can tell that for Mattie the dream still holds. He has no idea how to unsay the things he'd said. The last thing he wants to do is hurt her so he spins a new web of false hope explaining that first he has to look after his family, see them settled in the town, now the horse business is finished and then... and then... A sound from the saloon eventually saves him. It's Jed's unmistakeable high-pitched yelling. He runs.

The sight that greets him in the bar stops him dead. Jed is pinning a smartly dressed cattleman to the floor and screaming into his face; 'It's your sort damned near ruined our pa!'

Irwin moves in and hauls Jed to his feet. 'It's alright Jed, I'm here! What did he do to ya?' Jed says nothing, wipes his mouth, his breathing rapid, his eyes wild. Irwin pulls the man to his feet. 'What you do to my brother?' And Jed is there again, 'You cattlemen, driving your tic infested cattle by our pasture ... you killed our best...'

'Jed! Shut your mouth! What in hell's teeth..?'

'I introduced myself, real civil, asked him what business he was in, told him what business we was in... He laughed, they laughed! He called me country boy!'

'He knocked me off my stool!'

'He felled off! He pushed me! Pushed me away! Then he felled off, pulled me down with him, called me country boy!'

Much to Jed's annoyance Irwin apologises to the man, who he can see by his eyes has been drinking all day. He offers to buy him a drink which sets Jed off again. Irwin tells his brother to go and wait outside but he doesn't move. He guesses whatever drink Jed had taken has gone straight to his head. They hadn't eaten that day. He apologises again to the man explaining that they'd been riding for days and had failed to round up a single wild horse. These were stressful times. The man's name is Quinn, he's loud, drunk and vain – his concern for the muck on his coat overriding his annoyance. He's soon boasting about the success of his own cattle trading and Irwin can see exactly why his brother had taken against him. Quinn delights in telling them how they're in the wrong business and how you have to go with the times. He brags about how he's going to make a new fortune – not in cattle, not in *wild* horses, but in the draft horses – the thousands of heavy horses they're going to need in the cities and on the prairies, and how only he knows where they breed them, where you get two hundred dollar stallions that will make you twenty thousand dollars in Chicago – 'And it ain't in America!'

'And where would that be then, sir?' Jed quietly loads the question with sarcasm as he sulks on a stool.

'Well, I can tell you country boy, because it's somewhere you ain't never likely to go!'

Irwin knocks back his drink. The man is now seriously angering him. 'I wouldn't bet on that Mr. Quinn. Come on Jed, we got our own places to go.'

Quinn laughs, 'You have? How about France?'

They leave, Mattie is still waiting by the horses. 'So what's it to be Irwin?'

Irwin snaps, his belly feels hollow, he's angry as hell, 'Not now Mattie! I'll see you next time!'

She grabs him, 'You ain't leaving? Don't you dare!'

She's holding his arm in an iron grip. He relents and whispers in her ear. 'You remember that poem, *Parting is such sweet sorrow?'*

'Go on…'

Words now fail him. 'That's it…' She's still holding his arm. He kisses her. 'I gotta go.'

'Well you remember this… we ain't parting, you and I we's engaged!'

'How could I forget a thing like that?'

They kiss again, she loosens her grip, one more kiss and he heads off to the bank. Jed follows unable to resist a final excuse. 'It was your fault Irwin, all that at the bar… you telled me *when in town you hit 'em first and talk later.'*

'And that's how you get yourself hung.'

'Only if I stealed his horse!'

And Irwin finds himself laughing. His little brother maybe tall and lanky but he's still a boy trying hard to be a man. 'Come on we need to eat.'

Their final stop in town is the livery store. Irwin talks mustangs; how much they're fetching, if there's any coming down from Montana. He asks what buyers are looking for. He talks so long Jed gets bored; bored and depressed. Everything they're told confirms what Irwin had been telling him. The visit to the bank, his first, had been a sombre affair, then the dry goods store had refused them credit. It's overwhelming; talk of last year's bad harvest, farmers struggling, it was like the whole town was dying and they were dying with it. Unlike his brother he'd never worked away. His whole life had been spent on the farm, breaking in wild horses is all that he has ever known, if they can't do that what are they going to do? He keeps asking questions his brother can't answer. In fact Irwin's not even listening. He has stopped by a notice board. There's stock for sale, pictures of wanted men – rustlers and outlaws and the rewards for their capture. He reads an official notice; the government are releasing a million acres of Indian land in Oklahoma. He thinks about it… *a million acres…* But it's the small poster next to it that he removes, folds and puts in his jacket pocket. Jed asks what it is but gets no reply. Irwin is already moving on.

Once they cross the river and climb away from the plains the horses know they're heading home and there's purpose in their stride. There are now trees dotted around the hillsides and a rocky bluff that tells them they're nearly there. Jed becomes nervous, 'So what do we say to Pa?' Irwin tells him not to worry. To leave it to him. It's all going to be fine. He even looks like he believes it. Coming over one last rise they see the cabin and the barn ahead. A dog barks alerting the family. Horses in the paddock raise their heads and two young kids start to call across the valley.

Abe looks older than his fifty-five years. He too stares across the valley, but when the children call to him excitedly, telling him the boys are back, he doesn't move. He can see well enough and what he sees confirms the thing he most dreaded. He watches his sons as they ride in, their young siblings Luke and Martha running beside them. There are joyous shouts of *Where have you been? Why so long?* and *What did you get?* Abe comes slowly over as Irwin dismounts and calms them down. 'Now you two hold on there, I got something for everyone…'

'Horses? How about horses?' It's a rhetorical question. Irwin looks at his father but he's already turned and is heading for the cabin.

Inside Jed is full of tales for the little ones, spinning yarns of the sights he's seen and a fight he'd had with a drunk who assaulted him in the town. He'd seen a wagon train stretching for miles with hundreds of families heading West. And he'd seen Indians and black soldiers – a whole regiment of them on the move… Irwin is quietly glad to be home. He looks around the cabin, it has drapes on the windows, a clock above the fire and a buffalo skin over his father's chair. He's proud – they're all things that he had bought. He'd gone off working for a rancher when he was fifteen. The man had seen what he could do when he came to buy mares, paid him good money to break in his own stock. He'd stayed three years, come back on top of the world only to find that his mother was dying. It hadn't been the same since. A certain balance had gone, and his father was only half the man he was. Now this; a whole new heap of trouble. This is when his mother would steady the ship, smile, pray, trust in the Lord. Now there was only his older sister Mary-Ann, the antithesis of hope. She had hardly said 'hello' and he braced himself as they sat down for a meal. She had a way of capitalising on bad news, as though unhappiness was her only succour. He had a right to be as depressed as anyone but the all-embracing gloom with which she filled the room gives rise to a churning energy – a determination… but he tries to bide his time. It proves too much; first it's thanking the Lord for the tasteless food she's dumped in front of them, then they eat in a silence he cannot bear. He has to break it. 'Don't get down Pa… I got us a plan…' And that is Mary-Ann's cue, 'Don't get down? We're going to lose the farm!'

'No we ain't.'

'We are going to have to move to town.'

'Oh yeh! Like you always wanted!' This was the worst of it; not bringing back horses gave her the ammunition she had been waiting for. 'Don't listen to her Pa – she's been at you again ain't she?'

'No I have not – The bank's been at him again!'

'I talked to the bank! I've explained Pa!'

Abe shakes his head, wipes soup from his beard, 'You can talk to 'em all you like son, time's come we got to face facts. Even if you'd got us a hundred head…'

'We tried! They ain't there!'

'And if you had what would we do?'

Mary-Ann butts in; 'No one's come by while you was gone. Folks don't want 'em like they used to. *No one wants 'em*!'

It all goes quiet. The only sound is a quiet pretend-slurping as Martha feeds her new doll that the brothers had bought her. Jed looks to Irwin. 'That's what they was all saying in town, isn't that the truth?'

Irwin nods, 'We seen it with our own eyes. The move's to bigger farms, bigger machines.'

'Bigger horses…' adds Abe.

Irwin jumps up, 'That's right, that's right – *bigger horses* – now you're talking Pa! Bigger horses – and I know where you can get 'em!'

'Everyone knows where you get 'em.'

'Sure they do – they go to Chicago and they pay Chicago prices. Now we was talking to this trader in town…'

Mary-Ann mimics her brother, 'And he told us where we could get 'em for ten bucks!'

'Two hundred dollars instead of ten thousand!'

Irwin takes the crumpled poster from his pocket and smoothes it out on the table. It's an advertisement, dominated by an engraving of a large black draught horse. 'Look at this – this is what folks want now – Norman horses, can't get enough of 'em. Need 'em on the prairie, need 'em in the cities and you see this man here…' He points to the wording at the top of the poster, *R. M. DUNHAM, the world's largest importer and breeder of Norman horses.* 'This man Dunham, he's one of the richest men in the West and do you know why? Because he knows where they comes from.' He sits back down and faces his father across the table. 'Pa… there is only one place, one valley in the whole wide world where you can get these horses…'

'And you know that place!' Mary-Ann forces a sarcastic smile.

'I do.'

'And no one else in the world knows that place.'

'Except Dunham and this trader in town.'

Jed looks at his brother, wondering where this is heading. Mary-Ann goes back to eating her soup, confident that her brother's embarking on another of his crazy fantasies. 'There's only one problem Irwin.'

'There ain't no problem, Mary-Ann.'

'We don't even have two hundred bucks – we are owned by the bank!'

Abe throws down his spoon, 'No one owns me!'

'They do! You know they do!!'

He now brings his whole fist down on the table, 'No one owns me!!'

He gets up and heads for the door.

Irwin is the first to follow his father out, followed swiftly by Mary-Ann who is not about to let her silver-tongued brother have their father's ear without her being there. They both sense trouble, Abe had turned left out of the door and passed the window, he could only be heading for one place – the small, sod-built dug out that had been the family's first home. It had been used as a store for years, the roof proudly maintained by Abe, determined not to let his past be washed away. Now he's inside. They find him tugging at old feed troughs, throwing precious broken timber out of his way. Years of dust makes the old man cough as he fights his way into a dark corner. He takes a fencing spade and starts hacking at the bare earth. They watch, knowing not to interrupt. He digs like a man possessed, eventually clawing at the hole with his bare hands. He stops, hunched over, gathering his strength. Mary-Ann is sensing madness, Irwin is on a tightrope; *his father's never let them down...*

After an age where the only movement is the heaving of their father's shoulders and the only sound is the rasping of his breath, Abe reaches into the hole and clears away the earth around a piece of cloth. He frees it and pulls it clear. It's not very big, smaller than a feed sack. He shakes the dust off it, stands up and heads back to the house, saying nothing.

The family crowd round the table watching their father. The cloth turns out to be a bag. Out of the bag he pulls more of the same material, unstained by the dirt. It's like linen or sail cloth. It has pockets, it has buttons... He lays it out on the table as everyone starts to ask questions, 'What in tarnation..?'

Abe looks to Jed, 'Pick it up.' Jed hesitates, 'Go on boy, it won't bite ya.'

Jed picks it up, 'Oh my Lor' that's some weight!' Irwin grabs it from him, needing both hands to stop it dropping. He takes the weight and looks at his father. 'Pa?'

Abe takes the jacket back before Irwin can look further. He tells the youngest, Martha, to put her hand in one of the many little pockets. She won't, but Luke is straight in and his face lights up as he pulls out a coin. 'Oh my!!'

Mary-Ann pushes forward, 'Is that...?'

'That's a gold double Eagle.'

'Gold??'

The word echoes round the room. Irwin asks how many coins there are but Abe doesn't answer. He takes back the coin that they are now passing round. 'In Montana I struck gold...'

'You did – you did well!'

'Not that well. I saw other men, they got luckier than me but they lost it all; drunk it, whored it away, got robbed or got themselves killed. I promised your ma I'd come back with enough to buy us the land and that's what I did, it took half of what I'd got. He studies the coin, a friend he's not seen in a long time, then puts it carefully back in the vest. 'I had this made special. There was more losers out there than winners and if folks knew what you was worth they'd kill you soon as look at you.' He rests his hands on the cloth and closes his eyes like he's praying. 'So long as I've got this, no one tells me what to do, or how to live my life.' He opens his eyes and looks at each of his children. 'You understand?'

It was like those sudden changes in the weather; a violent wind blowing in from the north, a crack of lightning, the sky going black; everything was changed in a moment. No one was sure what was coming, but everyone was suddenly wide awake. Each one of the coins must have been worth twenty dollars and the entire vest was made up of tiny pockets. The younger ones had no idea what it meant but for Mary-Ann it meant moving to town, for Irwin it meant Norman horses and he knew it meant the biggest battle of his life. Mary-Ann had become the woman of the house with her mother's frugality and sense of order. Abe seemed to defer to her as he had to his wife. It appeared to Irwin to be a weakness, the lion frightened by the mouse; wrong! She wasn't a mouse, she was the pesky, bad natured little dog that never stopped snapping and yapping! 'Pa, listen to me Pa, you Know Ma said I was the best dressmaker in the county! You know we can't stay here! You have to think of Martha, you have to think of Luke; they need school! There's no Ma anymore to teach them letters and all those things she was good at. We can have a place right in the heart of town…' And like that pesky dog she was at his heels all day long and if Irwin tried to talk sense she was there, interrupting, doing him down, making such a noise that you couldn't think.

They had one mare in foal and Abe could tell she was near her time. Irwin sees his father leading her into the barn, follows him and seizes his moment, 'All we gotta do Pa is have us one good stallion and we have us a proper stud. Folks'll come from all over the state for that – we cover their mares…'

'Don't listen to him Pa.'

And she's somehow there, in the shadows like a silent killer. Pa tries to hold the line. 'You sure you can get the stallions?'

'You bet – I know where and I know when.'

'Of course he do – and he's going to ride 'em home – all the way from France!'

She doesn't relent, she's fighting for her life – any life away from here and she knows Irwin has one card that she can't play – their father's love of the place. He'd done it – he'd bought his own little piece of America; the land deed is framed on the wall. She hates it and she can feel her hopes drifting away every time Abe and Irwin speak.

'If I was to give you the Double Eagles…'

'No, no, no, you can't! You know he's a wastrel!'

'You telling me you have to go to France?'

'I hook up with a dealer I met in town.'

Mary-Ann laughs, 'You mean the drunk that had Jed on the floor?'

Irwin grabs his father's hand. 'I'd be looking for the future, like you did when you was young.'

'He didn't cross no ocean.'

'Grandpa did! It what's we do Pa – it's how you got this place and how we keep this place...'

Mary-Ann snorts, 'You, Irwin, ain't no Grandpa! I going to have to tell this Pa; Jed wanted to go to Montana, Irwin wouldn't go 'cause he has a girl in town…'

'I wouldn't go 'cus wild horses is history. I'm looking to the future here.'

'And how can he trust you? Where was you when Ma was dying?'

'Working! I was working…'

'He was in jail for fighting! Fighting over a woman he stole from an injun!'

The room goes quiet, Abe clearly unaware. 'Was that true?'

Irwin gives Mary-Ann a death stare. She smiles, triumphant, 'It's true as I'm standing here.'.

'It was a misunderstanding…'

The silence that follows reflects not the deed but the betrayal. What had Irwin done that was so terrible that he couldn't share it back home? What had he kept from his father? Abe won't ask, he walks away and carries on with his day. Bit by bit Irwin seeks him out and tries to explain, 'It was a long time ago... every kid has his wild time. I was younger then, I played poker, I know you told me *never*, so I never let on, but I found I was good... And I won me this squaw fair and square in a game. This guy said I cheated, they were cowmen, rough as they come, honest Pa – I only took 'em on to save the injun. If you could'a seen her, you'd a done the same. I was young, I didn't understand nothing, I'd won fair and square, cleaned the guy out – she was all he had left to gamble.'

'You didn't tell me.'

'I couldn't tell *Ma*, you know how she was about that stuff. Sheriff only put me in jail to save my neck.'

The problem was that that wasn't how he'd told it to Jed. *'I won me a squaw in a card game!'* He'd bragged about everything back then, *'Next thing I woke up in jail!'*... *'She wore nothing under that robe...'* Why Jed had then told Mary-Ann he'd never know, but somehow she always knew everything. She saw that as her role and the source of her power.

Another day and no one knows where they stand. Abe won't talk, he's keeping his own counsel. Mary-Ann knows she's played her trump card - her brother had a wild side, was always getting into scrapes, would never let the truth get in the way of a good tale and this French horse idea was his most fanciful yet. She bides her time, prepares more ammunition, is ready to remind her father of how her brother's not to be trusted. Through his teen years Irwin had often clashed with his father, they were like young bull, old bull but the older was still number one. She was quietly confident. Come the evening, finding him alone, watching the sun go down, she tries the soft approach, 'You alright Pa? I'm only thinking of you...'

'All you kids was born here, your ma raised y'all here, she died here. I could never leave this place, I'm sorry.'

Her heart sinks. She knows not to argue against her mother's memory and finds herself saying the opposite of what she means. 'That's okay. I understand.' Turning to go inside, she's face to face with Irwin, blocking the doorway. He smiles.

Her salvation comes the very next day. The dog barks as an old buggy approaches along the track. On board are two women. Irwin is the first to recognise them and their arrival leaves him open-mouthed. To make it worse they pull up right next to Abe as he repairs a broken fence. Irwin hurries over... 'Mattie!'

Her mother's driving the buggy, seeing her close-up she's the fiercest looking frontierswoman he's ever seen, skin like leather, eyes cold as stone and they're bearing down on him from the bare bones of a face. 'Is this the critter?' Her voice is like a dying-man's gurgle. 'He's promised he'd marry her, take her to California.'

Abe looks at Irwin, 'California?'

Irwin's staring at Mattie, 'Marry?'

Mattie looks like she's been crying for a week, she speaks through more tears, 'Admit It! You said you were through with Kansas! You said we'd go West, you promised!'

'If I could explain, I don't know that I used the word…'

'You promised!!' Mattie is now close to screaming, 'And Sally James, Sally James… I seen Sally James yesterday and she said you said exact same thing to her! Explain that!!'

'No, no, no…'

'Swear you didn't!'

'I swear!'

And now the mother, 'On the Bible boy – you come here and swear on the Holy Bible that you ain't mucking my daughter about.' From her pocket she produces the well-worn book. Irwin can only look to his father, 'Pa?'

'She needs to know Mr. Gurd. In my family a man that don't keep his word ain't no more use than a limping Longhorn and you know what we do with them?'

Before anyone can answer, Mattie is pointing a rifle at Irwin's face. 'We shoot 'em!'

Abe raises his arms, 'Now hold on there girlie… Put the gun down. Before anyone swears on anything, let me ask you Ma'am; you sure you want your daughter to marry a low down, two timing, silver tongued piece of prairie trash? You got a mighty pretty daughter there, 'tween you and me I think she deserves better.' Irwin stares at his father, is it a ruse? He can't truly believe…

The point is made, bit by bit the mood changes. In the end Irwin only has to swear never to go near Mattie ever again. Mattie gets her face slapped for crying, the buggy is turned round and the two women go back the way they'd come. The family watch them climbing away on the other side of the valley. Irwin thinks *close call!* Seeing the two-some arrive, hearing '*Marry...*' he thought she'd caught in the family way and he was about to be marched down the aisle. He can't help smiling. Abe sighs, 'When will you learn boy?'

'That girl should not be allowed near a gun, did you see her hand shaking on the trigger?'

'How many times have I told you?'

'I know.'

'First thing – if you wanna know what kinda wife a girl is going to make you, you look at her mother.' He goes back to working on the fence. 'I'm disappointed in you boy.'

For Abe it's confirmation of a deep fear – *so this is the way he goes on – the way he* ***still*** *goes on when he's away, even now he's twenty one?* Irwin had his mother's good looks and charm. It was a curse. Abe had always been rugged, thick set, had been surprised that his wife had taken to him – but she was never going for looks. She needed reliability, trust, faith in the Lord. He hadn't prayed since the day she died, refused to acknowledge so cruel a god. It was fickle nature he feared and he remained humble, knowing above all else that you needed luck in life and when luck comes your way, like it did for him, you need to keep your mouth shut. What had his son been doing? How many times had he told him to *think before you act!* He never did. The women flocked to him and it had given him a confidence, an arrogance that blinded him to the harsh reality of settler life – and his smooth words in turn blinded the women. What Abe saw that day was a generation of spoilt fools. In the evening he appears at the table again with the vest. Everyone crowds round. 'I've listened to you's all now, taken stock, put myself in the place of your Ma, thought what she would want for y'all. You're right Mary-Ann in what you said, she admired what you did, thought you was a mighty fine seamstress. Now I don't propose to let the bank get the better of us and before they do…' He puts his hands on the vest, '…there's enough here set you up…'

'No!! No Pa, you can't do that! You'll die in town!'

'It ain't about me anymore Irwin and it ain't about you – I gotta think about Martha, Luke, Mary-Ann. Do right by them like your ma would want. I gave her my word on that.'

'Pa I'm begging you!!'

But it was no good. Without new stock, with the market dead and the bank threatening, they needed to move and move fast. Abe had made up his mind. Mary-Ann's quiet barb is the final hurt before the lamps are doused. 'He doesn't trust you Irwin and that's all there is to say.'

Irwin roams the paddock in the moonlight, chewing tobacco, longing for drink, cursing the whole god-fearing family. As he sees it his sister was about to kill off a man's life's work, end a dream and for what, to make dresses?

Shortly after midnight Irwin makes his way to the barn. Jed is the night-watch, sleeping alongside the pregnant mare. Irwin touches his shoulder, the lad shoots awake, 'Has she started?' and he turns to the horse, struggling to get up but Irwin calms him down. 'Jed, we gotta go.'

'Go where?'

'I got the vest.'

'You what? No! Why?'

'It's what Pa wants.'

'No - he's going along with Mary-Ann.'

'That's not what he wants, you know that. He'll die in town. Pa's in a hole and we can get him out.'

'I ain't going against Pa!'

'Sometimes you have to – you heard that saying, 'The end justifies the means'?'

'More of your fine words! And look where they get you! Well no, no, I ain't with you on this…'

'So what you going to do – sew dresses?'

'If you wanna do this, whatever you doin', you talk to Pa.'

'I've talked, you know I've talked, the witch has made him deaf and now it's too late for that. They have sales over there and if we ain't there for the sales...'

'You're going to France?'

'I'm going to find that Quinn, he was heading for Abilene.'

'No!'

'Listen to me Jed, he's a cattle man – he knows nothing about horses, I know about horses, if I hook up with him…'

'He's a drunk!'

'He was drunk! We all get drunk - that don't mean he's a drunk all the time. Now come on…'

But Irwin is wasting his time. Jed can't believe that Irwin has taken the gold from under his sleeping father's nose. He watches in disbelief as he puts the vest on. His brother then takes a number of coins and puts them in the cloth bag. He gives it to Jed who is reluctant to even touch it. 'See, I ain't takin' it all. Sorry Jed, but you got the hard part now. You make sure you're all still here when I get back.'

It's like some kind of bad dream. Jed makes his way out of the barn and sees his brother riding off into the night. 'Irwin come back!'

TWO

Irwin had worked up the idea in his head that he and Quinn had something in common. Kansas was changing; the farmers were fencing off the land - they didn't want fifteen thousand head of cattle overrunning their pasture, spreading disease to their own animals. That's why the man was getting out of the game. Right now he would be waiting in Abilene for when his herd arrived off the trail. He'd do the deal with a trader from the East, the stock would be loaded onto trains and shipped off north to Chicago. Quinn was then heading straight to New York, to France and to the Spring sales. In Irwin's head he wouldn't be alone. He was sure that there were those in town would vouch for him; Abe's boy had a reputation for being good with even the feistiest of animals and what was more they'd tell how he could spot every weakness an animal could possess. He could make himself indispensable to the cowman. And he had money enough to buy his own stallion... He had it all worked out as he rode through the night, and arriving in Abilene, he could feel his luck was in – the place was wild with cowmen, some still drunk having been paid off at the end of the trail, one was auctioning off his horse in the main street, others were wating outside the barbers to get their hair cut and the women were out looking to do deals of their own. Someone fired off his gun, spooking the horses, turning heads, it was a place you felt anything could happen and Irwin headed out to the rail-yard determined to make it happen for him.

It wasn't what he expected, he'd seen the place before, he expected to hear the herds as he approached, expected the smell, the dust, the shouts of the men. It was eerily quiet, most pens were empty and men were cleaning up... He knew straight away; the train had gone. He asked around for Quinn. Found someone that knew the name, they suggested the hotel where he stayed. A desperate Irwin heads back there only to find the man had left. In an instant his plan is in ruins, *what was he thinking?*

As he takes his horse to be fed and watered it's like someone has pricked a bubble, *it was such a great idea!* Now the vest is no more than a great weight hanging from his shoulders. Back home they'll know by now what he's done. He heads for the saloon, trying to think of some way of not going back to the ranch, of not facing his father, of not facing his gloating sister, of not handing back the vest, of not feeling the shame that now engulfs him.

The bar's like a tinder-box, full of men who'd spent weeks in the saddle, who now have money to burn. The '*No Guns*' sign warns of what's to come. The noise level makes it difficult to think, the men's raucous laughter and celebratory yelling only serving to underline his own failure. At the bar, pressed between cattle-smelling bodies, he shouts for service and despairs of ever getting that drink. He can hear those next to him sharing their plans and suddenly he's listening - one of them's aiming to ride the next train West. *Train-hopping!* He'd done it before, it costs nothing, and it gets you wherever you want to go! Suppose he can catch a train East?

Soon he's riding fast as his horse will take him, a clear plan in his head. There's a homestead, middle of nowhere, Eileen, the daughter was called, sweet kid, he'd wished he could've stayed out there longer, but he'd only stopped by to do a trade. Well, it had stuck in his mind that she had done the darndest thing – she'd held up a sack by the railroad like a flag and the train had stopped – that's how they do the post out there – they took her parcel off her and carried on. Now, if she could stop the train again….

The family greet him, a welcome stranger, and they're keen to know the news, glad to hear that the cattle trade was dying out. Glad to hear that farmers were now banning cattle drives from their towns. They'd had a couple of deaths from Texas fever and didn't want anymore, life was hard enough as it was. Eileen cooks up a meal for their guest, wanting to ask him why he's come here, how come he remembered her name? Irwin simply explains his plan. How he's en-route to New York but missed his train. How he and his partner are heading for France to buy Norman horses. She thinks it all sounds wildly exciting. Her apparent enthusiasm encourages

Irwin but the more he talks, hears his own ideas spoken out loud, the more he can see his father staring at him... and the more elaborate his story becomes - like he's trying to convince himself it's going to happen. His father always shows his face when he's spinning yarns and the old man's words echo now in his head; '*The thing that marks out a true conman is his absolute belief in his own bullshit!*' It's not bullshit, it's going to happen! Irwin borrows paper and writes a note to his pa, promising he'll be back and save the business.

When the train's due he needs to sell his horse, 'Would you good folks care to do a trade?' The father's no fool. 'The last horse you sold me died.' Irwin shrugs, 'I'm sorry to hear that, he never did that when I had him!' He jokes but suspects he's met his match; it could be true or it's a ploy on the part of the farmer who knows Irwin has no choice. Only when they hear a far-off whistle do they finally agree a low price for the animal with saddle thrown in.

They can see the train in the distance, making its way across the endless flat grasslands. They head across the fields to where a wooden box lies next to the track. As Eileen raises her skirt to stand on it, she finds herself rising in the air. Irwin is behind her, his hands gripping her waist, he is lifting her high then placing her gently on the pedestal. He turns her and they are eye to eye. Before she can say anything he kisses her on the cheek and thanks her for her hospitality. He hands her the note he's written, kisses her on the other cheek then crosses the line. She can't speak, the train is now close. She holds up the flag, takes a small package and some letters out of her apron. Another blast of the whistle and in a great cloud of hissing steam the huge train slows almost to a halt. The conductor is hanging out from the steps on one of the carriages, he takes the parcel and letters from Eileen, then the train lurches forwards and moves on. She looks for Irwin assuming he was climbing aboard the caboose at the end. Her name is called and there he is hanging from the ladder between two wagons. 'See you when I get back Eileen!' She watches the train until it's almost out of sight; a tiny hope, a sadness and a longing.

Four days later, or maybe five - and as many trains later - it was all a blur, he arrives at pier 88 on the Hudson River in New York. At one point the absurd gamble looked doomed when he found the cattle train he was riding shunted into a siding to allow an express to pass; *Was that the end of the road?* It was the middle of the night, middle of nowhere and the train showed no sign of moving. He learned his lesson, jumped the train when it finally approached a town and paid to complete the journey on a wooden bench in third class. Exhausted as he is, his heart leaps when he's told the huge ship that towers over everything at the docks, is the Normandie – *Normandy!* It has to be the boat – and it hasn't sailed! The dockside is mayhem; thousands of people, many languages, everyone seemingly in a hurry – porters, passengers, dockers. Close-up the liner is even more impressive. It stretches as far as Irwin can see along the quay. He feels so near yet so far – the passenger gangways seem suspended in mid-air way above him and he can see that people are already boarding the boat.

He asks for help and finds some sort of departure office crowded with travellers and luggage. He clutches the battered valise that Eileen had kindly given him in exchange for his saddlebags. He uses it to push his way through and when he finally reaches the counter he explains that he's lost his business partner, name of Quinn, could they please tell him what cabin he's in? The man agrees to consult the manifest. Irwin doesn't know what that is, and becomes increasingly impatient as the man works his way meticulously through the hundreds of names asking for information Irwin doesn't possess – *How was he travelling; first class, second class, steerage?* He tells him to forget it and just sell him a cabin. To his horror he is told that all cabins are taken. He explains that it is absolutely vital that he gets on that boat, 'You don't understand - my life depends on it!' By now the clerk has made his own assessment of the dishevelled character in front of him, who smells faintly of cows and carries only a small bag. He directs him to another office where they might be able to help him. He makes his way as fast as he can through the mêlée, giving himself no time to think what he's doing but knowing it's now or never. The men hanging around in this next office look more like him, rough and ready and few are speaking

English. He queues for what looks like the ticket office. The man behind the glass has a heavy foreign accent and Irwin finds communication difficult. He doesn't understand what the man is asking him. Eventually he says to the guy as simply and slowly as he can 'I have to get to France! I don't care how!!' A short time later he's being seen by a foreign doctor and signed up to work his passage on the flagship of the Compagnie Maritime Transatlantique. He has no idea what he has done but as he follows the other men up a gangway and into the bowels of the ship he can't help but smile. He is shown into a shared windowless cabin with other men and finds himself collapsing on a bunk and laughing; he'd done it!! He was going to France! *How the hell did that happen?* It turns out that some of the old crew had jumped ship, having used it as a cheap way to get to America. He's happy to take their place. He says a thank-you prayer to his mother. She'd never judged him in life and in the long hours on the trains he'd prayed to her to help him. When he was at war with his father she was always a gentle forgiving presence in the background and he was sure she had to be with him now. He was euphoric, he didn't have to go back a failure, he was on the *Normandie* and there was only one place it could be going – Normandy – home of the Norman horse! He didn't need Quinn after all – he didn't even like the guy! If only Mary-Ann could see him now…

THREE

If the cabin was his new heaven, the fire room was hell. His job was stoking the furnaces that provided the steam to drive the ship's two enormous engines. The heat was overwhelming, the fire blinding and the noise in that metal coffin was deafening. He felt like he was half the size of the other stokers and at the end of the first shift the sweat had softened his hands and they were blistered and bleeding. His fellow grafters didn't smirk, they admired his grit. Someone was summonsed to bandage the one hand and he was reassigned to greasing the enormous pistons and other moving parts of the mighty engines. He was relieved, everyone worked almost naked in the boiler room and he had feared every moment that he was parted from his vest. He soon longed for daylight, to get up on deck and see where they were heading, but it wasn't allowed. One day he felt sick as a dog with the engine fumes and the rolling of the ship but he was told to get used to it. Eventually it passed and he started to work up all the stories he was going to tell when he got home – that he sailed on the most luxurious liner ever built – *a sailing ship with engines, 7000 horse power! That's a heck of a lot of horses! And they even had water toilets in the cabins!*

It was a good diversion because what would happen when the ship docked was beyond anything he could imagine. He got French crew members to teach him basic French words and one even knew about the horse sales. At this time of year the man reckoned that that was where the Americans on the boat would be heading. The news comes as a shock – so Dunham and Quinn weren't the only ones in the know? *Everyone on the boat?* Thinking about it he realised that it was only Quinn who had told him that no-one else knew and he had grasped at the idea as he tried to convince his family. It was all part of the ruse to get the gold. *Goddamn it!* But what the hell – he had the gold now and enough to buy a thoroughbred stallion. That's all he needed. He'd buy what he could and get it home somehow, even if he had to partner up with a blagger like Quinn. It was all going to be fine! When they weren't working or sleeping the men played cards and Irwin even manages to win some francs. As the boat docks in Le Havre, he picks up his pay - more francs and prepares to leave the ship feeling flush and on top of the world. Having no passport he wasn't supposed to go ashore at all, but one of the stokers tells him how it's done and way after all the passengers have disembarked he's joining crew members heading down a gangplank, mingling with all the dockworkers before slipping through a hole in the fence. He's wearing the one suit he'd brought, aiming to match up with Quinn and takes some time to adjust his eyes to the glare of the first daylight he'd seen in a week. *So this is France! Hell, I've crossed the ocean, hey Ma? I've done it, can you see me? Can you see me? I bet you can from where you are! I'm going to do you proud Ma, you wait and see!*

His crew mates had told him he was a long way from horse country and he'd have to get a train. That was okay, he had money, he could do that. He turns to look one more time at the ship – the biggest construction he had ever seen in his life. Its two funnels were still smoking gently and its four masts pointed naked to the sky. *I been on that, I made it go... Wish I could'a seen the sails, that would'a been a sight... Next time... I'll be on the deck... in a cabin maybe...* And he turns and walks hopefully to where he can see a steam train waiting by a platform. '*Le Perche...*' he has to ask for '*Le Perche.*'

FOUR

Abe's wet, rheumy eyes betray him sometimes especially when he's alone tending the animals. Irwin was the natural horseman, not him. The lad had somehow been at one with them since he was a babe. He'd talk to them and they always seemed like they understood, let him do things, trusted him. Now he'd gone and once again left his father all mixed up inside, missing him, remembering how he somehow always came good just when you were most mad at him. Headstrong fool - when you wouldn't let him go breaking another man's horses, he ran away – fifteen he was, only to come back with the finest string of mustangs ever seen. He said he'd paired up with the Cheyenne and you never quite believed him – wondered if there was some poor injun lying dead on the prairie. Where Irwin was concerned you never knew fact from fiction – because somehow he didn't either.

In the evenings now the age-worn father, who's not yet sixty years old, sits alone outside the cabin where he can look hopefully towards the horizon. Tonight a single tear escapes and runs down his cheek; brother Reuben, that's who Irwin was like. He was the wild one, he was the one, when they went West together, who never came back. That was always his fear when his son went away – would he come back safe? That was the only reason he'd said 'no' to him so many times – fear. The lad was too like Reuben and he couldn't stand to lose another. The image of his brother's death-white face, the lifeless corpse carried like some straw-stuffed doll, it was branded on his soul; shot for what? A game of cards? So many rivers of pain mingling now; his wife's choice - the wild one or the one you marry? She would never have married Reuben but he knew she had loved him and then along came Irwin like a reincarnation. He'd grown tall like Reuben, good looking with his mother's fine features, so, like his brother, he always attracted the women. There had always been a craziness he could never fathom – it didn't come from him and certainly not from his mother; was he even his child - had something happened when his back was turned? He hated himself for the thought. She was always the dutiful wife, a God-fearing Christian woman and he'd loved her with all his heart but there was a passion she had denied him and he could see it in the way she loved her son. Abe had been jealous and there was that one big question that would always be there, could never be answered. That was his burden.

****

If you've survived being lost in Nebraska you'll never feel lost again. That's Irwin's conviction. There you could ride for days if the weather turned, if you had no sun nor stars to guide you and you'd not see a soul to ask - and God help you if you found yourself in a forest. Here, hardly five minutes go by when you don't see a church steeple rising above the trees and as the little train makes its way through rich green valleys he feels his spirits rise – the landscape feels alive – people are working the fields, his sort of people and there are cattle, horses, sheep. He'll get along just fine here, he knows it. The railway worker had smiled when he asked for Le Perche, spotting instantly that he was American he had guessed where he wanted to go. The man spoke no English but indicated that Irwin had missed the train with all his compatriots on board. He had then written down all the details he needed to know – the town he was heading for was Nogent le Rotrou.

It takes several hours heading south - he clearly wasn't riding the express! He'd been ready with his bag, waiting at the door for the last three stations, afraid of missing his stop. Nogent... it's bigger than he thought, they passed factories as the train slowed down and the rail yard is busy. Outside the station a coach stands waiting with a wooden painted sign, *Hotel Soleil D'Or;* a hotel with its own coach? It could be expensive. He watches the other people who have got off the train, most are walking or being driven in one particular direction. He follows assuming it's the way into the town. It is, and the long main street is a revelation. It's not the stone buildings which have an ancient permanence, that stop him in his tracks, it's the more temporary ornamental arches that span the roadway – they are draped with both French and American flags and the whole street is lined with potted shrubs. He smiles, it's like a personal welcome! They must've known he was coming!

As he makes his way up the street, intrigued by the neatness of the little shops and men wearing smocks and clogs, he hears two American voices, women's voices... *there's American women here too?* It phases him slightly, the one is very finely dressed making him feel scruffy, making him hold back from introducing himself. He follows them up the hill. The younger of the two looks about Irwin's age, is more modestly dressed and listens intently as if being instructed. They turn in through a coach-arch. Irwin stops and looks up at the rather grand building. High up there's some type of fish carved into the ornate stonework and he can see that this building too is adorned with both French and American flags. He has to jump out of the way as a coach clatters through the arch. He hears more American voices as it goes past. Then he sees the sign *Hôtel Dauphin.* There's nothing for it – he has to go inside.

The lobby is quite modest. A man, who could be the manager, is busy answering a query from a guest and two children are on the stairs, one of them, a girl of about eight years of age is calling to attract the attention of the finely dressed woman who has just entered. 'Mama, Mama, Wirth says they don't have electricity!'

'Don't show off children, this isn't Chicago!' The woman turns and catching Irwin's eye, she smiles. He can now see that she is a natural beauty, with the look of a Southern Belle. He can only smile back and raise his hat to her. The man at the desk is now looking in his direction. 'Can I help you sir?' His English seems good, so that's a relief. Irwin approaches the desk, 'A room – I need a room.' The faintest of arrogant smiles crosses the man's face before it changes to apologetic, 'I'm sorry sir, the hotel is full.'

'Full? You stringing me along there?' The man looks at him, not understanding. Irwin had momentarily been caught out, thinking the guy was making a judgement. 'I need a room, sir.'

'Désolé, we have no rooms.'

Irwin steps back. He's annoyed with himself, he's not normally thrown by such a rebuff, but this is unfamiliar territory.

He makes way for someone else to approach the desk. This young man has a briefcase, takes out papers and converses with the manager in French. He hasn't a clue what they're saying but one word has him all ears, *'Dunham'? Did he say Dunham?* Irwin waits and the moment the conversation ends he is in there, 'Excuse me Sir, are you American?'

'Yes, I am.'

'Gurd, Irwin Gurd, good to meet you Sir.'

'Charles Stephenson'

The fact that the man seems to be about Irwin's age gives him confidence, although he looks more like some kind of bookish student than a trader. 'Can you help me here; I need a room, and I think there's some misunderstanding – the gentleman says they are full up.'

'Oh dear.' He turns to the manager and they speak in French. He turns back to Irwin, 'He's very sorry but it's the sales – all the hotels in town are full.'

'All the hotels? Well that ain't so smart you know? I've come four thousand miles; what am I supposed to do – go home?'

Charles commiserates, suggesting that all Irwin can do is hope for a cancellation or for someone to have missed the boat. He is about to continue on his way when Irwin stops him. 'Charles... Mr. Stephenson, sir, did I hear you say the name 'Dunham''?

'Indeed you did – he's the gentleman I work for...'

'You work for Dunham? You're kidding me?'

'I'm afraid not. He's in the salon right now with Mr. Ellwood.'

'Ellwood? Well there you go, that's another name that sounds kinda familiar to me...'

Charles leans forward, he himself quietly impressed to be in such company, 'The steel magnate? Barbed wire?'

'The barbed wire guy, oh my! Of course! Charles I have got to stay here!'

'Well good luck!'

And he goes on his way.

Irwin is soon back at the desk and with persistence discovers that there are some guests who have yet to arrive. They are due later in the week on the Cherbourg boat, so the poor manager is forced to admit that yes, statistically it is possible there could be rooms that are not taken. However he is unwilling to offer them to Irwin on that basis.

Irwin retreats into the hotel yard. He's angry, feeling that he is being judged by the way he looks. Somehow he needs to have a shave, smarten himself up. He stuffs his battered hat into his valise. He's angry because if they knew what he was worth right now they'd sure as hell judge him differently. One Double Eagle and he could have the best room in the hotel, well, not the best, there's clearly big money here, but at least he could have a bed. However he'll not squander a cent. He's here now, he's made it. It's all to play for… but when the hell is the sale? If some folks aren't even arriving for a week?

He wanders round the yard, not sure what he's looking for – he can smell the kitchen, maybe there's also a wash-house of some sort? He's approaching a door when suddenly it opens and a girl shrieks in surprise. 'Can I help you?' She's nearly dropped the tray of crockery she's carrying. Irwin apologises; he's just having a look around.

'Are you losing someone?'

'No, no, no…'

'Okay!'

And she carries on followed by another two girls also carrying trays of crockery. They head off through the coach-arch and out into the street, giggling, the other girls imitating the one's attempt at speaking English.

Next Irwin tries the stables, most of the horses are out but he's drawn to one that looks to him surprisingly like a mustang. He can see it's nervous and whispers to it, calming it down until it lets him stroke its mane. He expects to see a stable-lad but there's no one around. He looks through a door at the far end of the stalls. He's in luck – it's a tack-room and it's where the coachmen change into their livery. There are clothes hanging on hooks, there's a tap and everything you need to groom both horses and men.

It's early evening when Charles Stephenson comes downstairs, dressed for dinner and heading for the salon. The first voice he hears is familiar and on entering he sees a clean-shaven Irwin, one arm resting on the fireplace, holding court in front of two finely dressed couples. He is particularly addressing the attractive woman he'd encountered earlier in the lobby. She is smiling, enjoying his tale.

'You can ask my father Ma'am - he'll tell you - no one in the whole of Kansas or Nebraska has a better eye for a horse than I have. I even ran away from home for a horse.'

'You did not?'

'I was fourteen years old. This fella could see I was good with 'em, he said, "I want you to break me some wild horses." I said, "I'm sorry sir, wedon't call it like that - sure; I'll gentle_'em for you..." I had to explain to him - a broken horse is a slave - you can never trust him; a gentled horse is your friend and he'll follow you for the rest of your days. Heck gentlemen, you wouldn't break a woman would you?'

There's a ripple of polite laughter. The woman looks to her husband, 'Mark?'

'Wouldn't dream of it my dear.'

Mark Dunham touches his wife's arm as he looks reassuringly into her eyes. He looks about fifty, but that could be the thick black moustache ageing him. He seems quite at home in this foreign place, a well travelled man of the world. Irwin likes that, that's how he sees himself, a little further down the line. Like his wife Dunham exudes confidence and warmth. Irwin had taken to the couple immediately. They seemed to have no airs or graces, had welcomed him and were enjoying his company.

Charles had entered quietly and taken a seat further back in the room amongst other American guests. His presence had not gone unnoticed by Irwin, 'Mr. Stephenson…' Charles is embarrassed as all eyes turn upon him. 'Mr. Gurd…'

Irwin notes the innocent discomfort. He knows at that moment that Charles is going to be a useful young guy to have around. The other couple Irwin had been addressing seem more reserved and questioning of Irwin's presence. Ellwood is older with a full beard and eyebrows that give him a permanent frown. Chit chat clearly isn't his bag, he's here to do business. 'So how big is your outfit young man?'

'Nothing like the size it's going to be when I'm through buying me stallions over here.'

'How many horses?'

'The number varies of course…'

'Were you at Chicago?'

'Chicago? No sir I was not at Chicago. I can sell every horse I got without crossing the county line'

'A hundred head, two hundred?'

Carrie Dunham can sense the way the conversation is going. She comes to Irwin's aid. 'Mr. Ellwood had six hundred horses at the Chicago show.'

'Six hundred?'

'I did and a hundred grooms in livery…'

'A private train for the horses.' Carrie gives Irwin the eye - *you have to act impressed!*

'A private train? Then I'd better get me two trains… I'm a little behind you for now sir…' he mumbles, 'Hundred, two hundred head depending… But have you gentlemen seen those McCormick reapers, they take some pulling I tell you – twenty horses to a hitch…'

And Dunham is with him, 'That's right, now they're opening up the prairies.…'

'The market gentlemen is as big as the grasslands themselves!'

'That's absolutely right!'

And a murmur of agreement spreads round the room.

'So, hell yes, I'll see you there in Chicago Mr Ellwood Sir, look forward to the day!'

Irwin can't believe his luck, *Well how about that Ma?* He still has the Dunham poster in his pocket, like some invitation to a ball, but here he was with the man himself - he'd walked right in without the need of a ticket! Now he was following the couple up the street going who knows where? Charles was with them with his little briefcase under his arm. Irwin felt that Charles was the key to this whole thing. He could ask Charles when the sale was taking place; where do you find the horses? All those things he needed to know. He was part of a flow of people all heading in the same direction, the hotel workers hurrying past with a sense of urgency. *'I'll see you there in Chicago, Mr Ellwood sir!' – Did I really say that?* Irwin is quietly smiling all the way to the top of the rise where the road opens out into a square with a fountain. He can hear singing coming from inside a grand, stone-fronted building adorned with yet more flags. Some local men are chatting in groups outside. He can hear the odd American voice. He looks around wondering if he might see Quinn, but the Dunhams go straight in and Irwin follows, not wanting to lose sight of them. They seem to know where they're going and head through into a large hall. It's a chaotic scene. The singing is coming from the local firemen who are having a final rehearsal of the National Anthem, conducted by a fat man wearing a sash. One of their number arrives late and joins in as he makes his way through the hall. The place is set out for a banquet, and the girls he'd seen in the hotel yard are busy with others making final preparations. Irwin watches the Dunhams being welcomed by a smock-clad gentleman. They talk before he shows them to the long top table. It's noisy as voices echo round the room. Irwin makes his way slowly between the tables, nodding to various people, noting the number of Americans, but Quinn is not amongst them. Charles is sitting down and taking papers from his case as the Dunhams stand around being introduced to various dignitaries. Irwin casually pulls out a chair and sits at the table next to Charles. Charles is concentrating hard on something he's reading and doesn't seem to notice. Irwin surveys the room realising yet again just what a big deal this horse business is. Charles looks up nervously from the typewritten piece of paper, noticing Irwin for the first time. 'Mr. Gurd…'

'Irwin, please… call me Irwin. A fine gathering…'

'Indeed…' He takes a handkerchief and wipes sweat from his brow.

' So tell me, Mr. Stephenson, how do you fit into this business? You a horseman?'

'No, no, to be truthful, I feel like a bit of a fraud.'

'A fraud?'

'I know nothing about horses.'

'I didn't think you looked the part – so what line are you in, Charles, can I call you Charles?'

'I'm a banker.'

'Oh wow! How d'you get into that?'

'My father, he owns the bank. He's a friend of Mr. Dunham's and he thought this would be a beneficial experience.'

'Oh my, I wouldn't mind the experience of owning a bank! Maybe we should all swap around!'

At this point other guests arrive at the table. A French woman sits down next to Irwin and offering a polite 'Bonsoir,' continues to introduce herself in French. Irwin, understanding not a word, nods and manages a 'Soir.' She, receiving no answer to the question she's just asked, smiles awkwardly into the distance before looking away down the table. Then, like someone has given a signal, people in the body of the hall start to take their seats. The Dunhams sit next to Charles, the town mayor and other dignitaries all take their places along the table. There's a commotion at the one end. A man in uniform who turns out to be the Chief of Police is remonstrating to a flustered little man in a suit who Irwin has seen earlier bossing all the hotel girls. The little man looks along the table, counting the places. Irwin engages Charles in conversation, 'You been here before? This your first time?' He doesn't listen to the reply. The little man is haranguing the first girl Irwin had encountered in the hotel yard – the one who'd nearly dropped her tray. She is now looking along the table, counting the places. She looks at Irwin, he smiles – *she's beautiful!* The little man pushes her and she hurries off while he provides another chair for the police-chief's wife. The girl soon returns with another place setting. Irwin smiles at her as she passes. There's a tear in her eye and she turns angrily away.

Irwin starts to relax as the choir opens the banquet with the Marseillaise. There are bottles of wine on all the tables, people seem to be helping themselves so... *This is the life!* He pours himself a glass as everyone claps the firemen, the mayor welcomes his American guests and the waitresses start to serve food. Irwin can't believe his luck. Course after course is set before him – there's sea-food, there's salads, there's cold meats, there are other things he's never seen nor tasted in his life but he's not complaining, this is the first proper meal he's had since the boat and that had been vile. Charles meanwhile seems distracted, hardly eating a thing and mumbling silently to himself. He doesn't even attempt the meat course that Irwin suspects might be a rather hairy section of cow's tongue, then two more courses, also avoided before the table is banged and he grabs Irwin's arm. Irwin asks if he's alright, there's no answer; Dunham is rising to his feet and after a few words in French from the mayor, he starts to address the hall. 'Monsieur Mayor, Monsieur Perriot, Monsieur Tacheau, I bring you greetings from Washington, from Secretary Simpson and from Senator Coburn of the Kansas State Board of Agriculture....' He stops and looks to Charles. Charles rises to his feet and begins to translate Dunham's words into French. Dunham then continues. 'You will be pleased to know that your Percheron horse is now the number one draft breed in the United States, it is the most sought after by farmer and teamster alike, they will travel any distance and go to any lengths to get them. The Percheron is indeed the horse that powers America!' People clap and as Charles continues to translate Irwin wonders why he and his pa hadn't cottoned on to this earlier. They'd nearly missed the boat! The family should be thanking him, *if I hadn't come over...* More applause and Charles finally sits back down, his job done. Carrie Dunham leans across and congratulates him as he wipes his brow yet again. 'Didn't he do well?' she says to Irwin. 'He certainly impressed me Ma'am!' and Charles smiles for the first time that evening. He pours himself a glass of wine and knocks it back in one. He's now a different person, 'Did it sound alright?'

'Sounded very French to me. That's a heck of a lot of horse dealers out there Charlie!'

'With a lot of American dollars Mr. Gurd! More this year than ever apparently.'

Irwin's hand slips inside his jacket. He can feel the vest making him sweat. *American Dollars, Double Eagles…* So many questions, he is not sure where to start, but Charles is in talking mood now and he's soon learnt that the actual sale of the horses takes place at a grand show in a couple of weeks' time when medals will be awarded for the best in show. In the meantime the buyers tour the farms, meet the leading breeders, go to Paris, see the sights, make the most of the trip. Charles has assumed that Irwin has found accommodation and is disturbed to learn that he has nowhere to stay. Irwin insists it's no big deal. He undoes the bandage on his hand and discreetly shows Charles a large weeping welt across his palm. 'See this…?'

'What in heaven's name?'

'Shh… Between you and me Charlie, I'm lucky to be here at all… We had us a barn fire back home; this was trying to save my ma…' He holds the hand where Charles can see it. 'God rest her soul! It was not to be, it spread - I lost not only my ma… Lost my clothes… everything but what I'm standing up in… but I knew for the sake of my pa, my brothers, my little sister, I had to get here – This is our only hope!'

'You lost your mother?'

'I'm doing this for her, so you see if I have to sleep the night in a corn crib…'

'The stables? You can't sleep in the stables! I'll talk to Mr. Dunham…'

'No, no! Please don't tell a soul, I don't trade on sympathy.'

'But he could talk to the hotel, they could even put another bed in my room, I don't care!'

'No, no…'

'The room is big enough!'

'Then I'll gladly sleep on the floor. That'll work – just for tonight! Thank you – you got a good heart, you know that?'

'Well…'

'You see – the Lord looks after his own! Thank you Jesus!'

Charles, loosened now by the drink, can't help smiling, 'That's funny!'

'It is?'

'In Chicago we have a saying, *The devil looks after his own.'* And he chuckles to himself.

Irwin reckons his new room mate is not that accustomed to alcohol. As the evening progresses, Charles is called on to interpret various of the Dunhams' social encounters and he's not helped by the variety of spirits that are passed around the tables. Irwin can detect a slur and see his room-mate's increasing struggle to understand the French. He makes a note that something like *répétez s'il vous plait* is a phrase worth remembering. The air becomes thick with tobacco smoke. The noise level rises and singing breaks out on the floor of the hall culminating in a sing-off as an American delegate, rising to the challenge of a fireman singing the Marseillaise, stands on a table and breaks into the Star Spangled Banner. Charles too rises, hand on heart and falls against Dunham who is not impressed. Irwin steps in, assuring them he'll be okay and offers to see him back to the hotel. Carrie is grateful, and watches them weave their way through the rowdy crowd. There is something about Irwin that intrigues her.

He has also caught the eye of a man who, like some civil-war beggar from back home, touches Irwin's arm as he passes, 'Excusez-mois monsieur…' The man has a limp and a scar on the side of his face. His accent pushes the sound to the back of his throat. Irwin keeps moving, wanting to see his charge in the open-air before he is sick. The limping man follows, introducing himself as they reach the door. 'Forgive me monsieur, I don't remember you …'

'You don't, so?'

Irwin is wary and keeps walking, holding firmly to Charles's arm.

'Everyone else on your table I know from last year – Monsieur Dunham. Monsieur Ellwood, they are my friends… but you Sir…'

'Gurd, Irwin Gurd and you are?'

'Maurice Valmy. If I can be of assistance while you are in le Perche…'

'That depends on your business. Like Mr. Dunham and Mr. Ellwood I'm in the market for stallions'.

‘Then you have come to the right man.’

At this point Charles, refreshed by the cool evening breeze, breaks into another chorus of the Star-Spangled Banner and heads off towards the fountain. Irwin follows with Valmy close behind. He keeps up with them, assuring Irwin that he knows all the top dealers. He sticks with them until it is agreed that he should come to the hotel in the morning and they can talk. Irwin is suspicious, he has plenty of experience of dodgy operators but is happy to milk this character for whatever knowledge he possesses. It’s a way in, it’s all good, it’s been a great night. He guides Charles away from the square towards the hotel, as his charge enquires if they’re still in France. ‘You bet we are Charlie!’

And it looks like I’m going to get me that stallion Ma!

FIVE

Irwin wakes early to the sound of a distant tinkling bell. There's a dull ache in his head. He remembers an apple brandy burning his throat, maybe that was the culprit. He throws back the blanket and gets up off the floor. Charles is still out-cold, exactly where he collapsed the night before, fully clothed, onto the bed. Irwin covers him up. He sees the room for the first time; big, bold patterned wallpaper – it seemed to be on every wall throughout the hotel. There's a dressing table with a mirror and the biggest, most ornate wardrobe he'd ever seen. He can't resist a peep inside. Charles's clothes are hanging on a rail. He has a moment of panic; his own clothes are neatly folded up as a pillow. He drops to the floor and checks – at the bottom of the pile is the vest. He can breathe. The tinkling bell sounds again, nearer this time. He goes to the window. A young girl is driving a number of goats down the street. A woman comes out of the building opposite and the procession stops. Irwin watches as she milks the goat and fills the woman's jug. He watches her hands, he can feel her natural connection to the animal, to the earth. She then carries on her way down the street. *I love this place!*

He's walked the town, grabbed and eaten a stick of bread from the baker's and is sitting having coffee in the salon when the Dunhams walk in. He explains that Charles has tried to move but the pain in his head was such that he couldn't even sit up. Carrie exchanges a guilty glance with her husband and explains that Charles's parents are Quakers and he has led a very sheltered life. They had entrusted their only son to their care, hoping the trip would broaden his experience; she didn't think what happened to him last night was what they had in mind. Mark Dunham thinks it's the best thing that could have happened to him and is starting to talk horses with Irwin when Monsieur Valmy appears in the doorway. Irwin excuses himself before he can be embarrassed by the man's presence.

Valmy takes Irwin off the main street to a small bar. Little glasses of pastis are placed in front of them and Irwin gets straight down to business, 'I have to tell this Mr. Valmy; I have to go home with something *real special*. You understand what I'm saying here? There ain't no room on my boat for old plugs or half decent mares; I need stallions; I need the biggest and *the best.'*

'Monsieur, monsieur, do not insult me; you are talking to Maurice Valmy - I deal only with the best.'

'And with respect Sir; how do I know that?'

'Look at me - I was left for dead in the Africa war. If you are perfect in this life, the struggle is hard, if you are like me, they say *impossible*. I make a life, you know how I do it?'

'How?'

'By working harder, being better at anything I do.'

'I'll drink to that!

'Salut!'

They knock back the pastis and Irwin takes in this damaged character as he rummages in his pocket with a three fingered hand. He's known plenty of war veterans, his heart has always gone out to them whatever side they were on; not needed anymore, not perfect, not wanted. Valmy produces a cigar and offers it to Irwin with a light. He puts his hand in another pocket and retrieves a half-smoked nub. Irwin takes note, but presses on; 'So tell me… I heard there's two hundred dollar horses out here that would cost me thousands of dollars back home.'

Valmy looks at him and snorts, 'Who told you that? You say you want the best?'

'Only the best.'

'Then I am for you. The best stallion, the best price – a fraction of what you would pay back home, but not two hundred dollars! Two hundred dollars?' He snorts again and bangs his empty glass on the counter. The patron comes and fills it up. As he does so a number of men wearing smocks and clogs come into the bar and stand next to Irwin. They're short and stocky with farmer's hands. They chat in indecipherable French to the patron. Irwin catches the eye of one of them who gives him a cold stare; *a drunken stare?* It's still early morning… Valmy nudges Irwin's arm and starts to move away to a table with their glasses. The man follows, grabs Valmy and shouts angrily in his face. Valmy shrugs him off and explains to a surprised Irwin, 'He's a drunk, ignore him.' But others in the bar start joining in the hostility, throwing angry comments their way. 'He's getting them all going now - farmers! Never satisfied!'

'What's going on?'

'They're blaming me for ruining them – me!!'

'How are you supposed to be doing that?'

'Talking to you – going to the dinner last night. Selling their precious horses to foreigners.'

In no time Valmy and Irwin are surrounded by angry locals and some of them are now shouting directly at Irwin.

'What have I done? I ain't done nothing, I only just arrived!'

'You're American, that's enough – you dump your cheap wheat …'

'Cheap wheat? Gentlemen we can't help that, you should see where it grows – best soil in the world they reckon! Tell them that!'

Valmy insists he won't say that, but continues to translate as every farmer competes to make their point. 'They say you ruin them, you subsidise your farmers, seven francs a bushel, is that right? They know their stuff, but they are stupid. Le Perche is not good soils for wheat – they should go for livestock, but then the only ones getting rich here are the stallioners, the men that have first call on the best horses. Désolé, I think we picked the wrong bar.' The hostility continues as the farmers even argue between themselves. 'Perhaps we go...'

Outside Irwin's doubts about Valmy are compounded. The contrast between the warm welcome the Americans received the night before and this backstreet hostility confirms to him that this is not the company he needs to be in. On top of that Valmy is now digging away at his finances. He says if Irwin tells him how much he is prepared to spend, he will go off and find the horses. That is not the way he wants to play it. He claims he has to be back at the hotel – he has other meetings arranged. Valmy follows him all the way back but luckily doesn't come inside. Irwin hangs around in the lobby, he has no idea what his next move will be.

He finds a remorseful Charles in his room. Part of him is panicking and part of him keeps drowning under waves of nausea that leave him wanting to die. He should be accompanying the Dunhams on a trip out of town but can't stand without the room swimming. Irwin takes him outside to get some fresh air. He dips his head in a bucket of water. The poor man is still wondering what happened. 'You mixed grape and grain, don't worry about it. You're still alive ain't you?'

'I'd rather be dead. What have I done? Did I make an ass of myself?'

'No, no… you never hit a soul, and you sang pretty good…'

'I sang?'

Attempts by Irwin to move on and find out information about changing money, banks, buying livestock, all fall on deaf ears as Charles sinks into a swamp of shame and regret. 'Do you think they'll tell my father?'

Irwin could not care less. Mention of *fathers* is a stab wound he can do without. He can see his own father, the careful man who would never gamble – never went into wheat because you never knew when you planted the grain what tricks nature would play. He'd survived when other sodbusters had fallen prey to drought. He'd buried his security in the earth, taken every precaution *and what have I done?*

The *haves* and the *have-nots* – he'd learnt this morning that it's the same the whole world over and here he is taking the biggest gamble of his life, balanced between the two with no idea how to tip the scales.

The Dunhams appear in the early afternoon and their arrival in the yard causes quite a stir. The open carriage they are in is pulled by two magnificent black horses. Irwin had kept a keen eye out for the local breed since his arrival. He could spot the distinguishing features – a thick neck, strong hindquarters, but until this moment he had not seen anything remarkable – the breed seemed to come in all sizes but this pair were huge, with a stunning wavy mane hanging down the one side of the neck. They must have been special because the staff were coming out into the yard to admire the spectacle.

Dunham can see that Irwin is impressed. He explains to him that one of the breeders has loaned them to him for the duration of his stay. They are the stuff of heroic statues in town squares, they're even better than the idealised image on Dunham's poster. They're the Holy Grail that you search for but don't expect to find. 'This is what I've come for Mr. Dunham, this is exactly why I'm here!' Irwin is six feet tall but still finds himself looking up into the horse's eyes. Charles is standing nearby trying to appear normal. Irwin grabs him, unable to control his excitement; 'Now you see why we're all here – ain't they beautiful?'

'Well, indeed, they're big…'

'Big? Big ain't the half of it! I'm going to have to educate him here Mr. Dunham, Sir!' And he leads a slightly reluctant Charles round the horses. 'This is a good, working stallion. And do you know how you tell? You look from the back... This is the engine... You look at the hocks here - look! Worst fault at a glance is crooked hocks; you're looking for power Charlie! That means good bone and plenty of it.'

Dunham concurs as he helps Carrie Dunham out of the carriage. He tells Irwin that Monsieur Perriot, the breeder, raises the finest Percheron stallions in the world and that's why he comes back to him year after year. He is delighted that Irwin appreciates the breed like he does. He takes his wife into the hotel. She stops to ask Charles if he's feeling better and mouths a discreet '*thank you*' to Irwin for looking after him.

Two of the kitchen girls have come over to see the horses as the stable lad comes and uncouples them from the carriage. Irwin recognizes the one in particular. He says a friendly 'Hi there, how you doin'?' and apologises – he admits that he was the one at fault at the banquet and he's sorry if he was responsible for her getting into trouble. She ignores him. Irwin assumes it's a language problem. 'She don't understand.' The girl turns on him, eyes blazing. 'I understand, I understand very good!'

'You speak English?'

'Yes I speak English.' And she says something clearly

derogatory to her friend in French. Irwin asks Charles to translate but before he even has time to work it out the girl is on the attack, 'You! You could have losed me this work, I could lose job because of you!'

'No? If you want me to have a word, explain….'

He touches her arm, she shrugs him off and turns to go back inside. She stops by the door, 'And you are wrong!'

'Wrong? About what?

'Les chevaux; You tell him you look from the back.'

'That's right.'

'Wrong – you look from the front…'

'No!'

She comes back and talks to Charles, 'First thing, you look in the eye – everything about him, you see in the eye.' She looks at Irwin. He smiles at her. 'Yes? No?'

'You're talking about disposition – a clear eye, a big eye…'

'Tell you everything! Who he is…' She comes to Irwin, 'Look in the eye, you know the horse.' The look she's giving him throws him for a moment. It's like she knows too much about him already.

'Well… his disposition… that's correct…'

'If you can trust him. If he is crazy, stupid.'

'What's your name?'

She turns and walks off to the kitchens. Her friend follows, smiling at Irwin, 'Jacqueline, elle s'appelle Jacqueline.'

Irwin hangs around with the horses, watching them being fed and groomed. He even offers to help, but there's a language barrier and he can't find out any of the information he needs to know. He's kept one eye on the yard and kitchen door whenever he's heard female voices; he liked that Jacqueline, she was one fiery kid and unlike the lads in the stable she spoke his language and she talked horses! She doesn't show her face again and he's quite depressed when he makes his way to Charles's room to face up to his next challenge; where's he going to sleep? Charles is now finally feeling human again and has news. He is so grateful for everything that Irwin has done for him that he has arranged for him to have his own room. No one else need know, it's a private arrangement between the two of them. 'You've paid?' Charles nods; there was no need for Irwin to be vulgar, that's what *private arrangement* means. 'They told me they had no rooms…' Charles shrugs and moves onto to other business; Mr. Dunham wanted to know if Irwin had any experience with mustangs?

It's to be an early start and there's a lot of activity in the hotel as Irwin makes his way down from his room the next morning. The Dunham children are racing around with their young chaperone trying to calm them down. It's busy in the yard with horses and coaches being prepared for the day ahead. There are many American voices, but Irwin avoids conversation. He's comfortable with the Dunhams, but is wary of those, like Ellwood, who ask too many questions. He now knows that he was right – it was a mustang stallion he'd seen in the stables. Dunham has had it shipped all the way from Illinois as a gift for a business associate. He's asked for Irwin to be around as he's nervous about the animal's temperament. He has good cause to be; as Irwin watches the Percheron stallions being hitched to the carriage there's a commotion inside the stables. Men are shouting and there's the unmistakable sound of horse kicking wood before the mustang careers out of the building dragging a young stable boy who is desperately holding onto the halter. Irwin shouts, 'Let him go!!' Whips crack and people scatter as the frightened animal runs amok in the yard. It's sometime before Irwin can ward off the stable lads, take control and calm the horse to a point where it lets him lead it around. Dunham thanks him. 'I warned them he was wild.'

'He ain't wild – if he was wild he'd a kicked everyone of yous by now! He's spooked that's all – he's a long way from home, a long way from those that speak his lingo.'

Carrie Dunham is impressed, 'Those folks back home, you told us about, they were right – you have a gift with horses.'

'I learnt their language that's all – once you speak the same language, you understand each other – you know that?'

Dunham asks if he thinks the animal will be okay if it's tethered to the carriage for the morning's ride. Irwin shakes his head, *not a good idea!* He thinks it will be better if he comes with them and rides the horse alongside. That way he can talk to it, let it know it's going to be just fine. Carrie outdoes her husband in her gratitude, 'That is so kind! But don't you have other business to attend to?'

'Nothing that won't wait. What sort of gift will you be giving if he kicks off soon as you hand him over? He's been through enough already – they're herd animals you know? He's been taken from his family, shipped half way across the world. I need to let him know it's goin' to be just dandy.'

By the time the tack has been sorted and Irwin is satisfied the horse is saddle trained, a crowd has gathered making the animal nervous. 'You see – this here's a country horse, not used to all this – he's itching to go Mr. Dunham.' He has to keep a tight rein as the Dunhams and Charles climb into the carriage. As the party moves off Irwin spots Jacqueline and her friend and can't resist heading over, 'See this – pure American stock - You look in the eye! Tells you everything you need to know!' He loosens the rein and the horse is off at a gallop, through the arch and up the street. Jacqueline is left standing there, trying to fathom this young man who is nothing like any other American she's met in the three years she's worked at the hotel. An angry call from the kitchen summons her back to work.

SIX

There have been many mind-blowing experiences since leaving home, from riding the rail-road, to being lost in Manhattan with its towering buildings that leave the streets in shadow; the million people, rich and poor, the horses, street railways – all competing with you for space as they head who knows where? He didn't too much care for that. Then there was the never to be forgotten week on the Normandie – how could they build anything so vast, so magnificent on the outside, hot and noisy as steel-coffin-hell down below? So much had happened in so short a time, the images coming back as Irwin, happy to be back in the saddle, follows the carriage for more than an hour before it stops at a roadside inn. 'Auberge' says the sign painted on the side wall. Then, people and horses refreshed, the party continues on for a real long ride, stops at another auberge before they do the same all over again. At each stop the Dunhams ask how he's doing. He's doing fine, and more to the point, so is the mustang although Irwin worries about what sort of future lies in store for the poor animal. But Irwin's having the time of his life, enjoying the difference all around him; the types of coach and horses that race past them heading the other way – the springing, he thought the springing on the coaches looked real fancy. And then the things that are the same the whole world over – the old farmer on his mule cart who won't be hurried and holds up the traffic. Then the age of everything; the villages they pass through, the buildings and even the people they pass; women heading for market, a young girl leading a cow who knows where? They all look like they've been around forever. Why so different? Is it the energy? They all seem slow. Is it *his* energy? Back home there was a driving force; the urge to make something happen or die. Hunt the buffalo 'til they're gone, round up the wild horses 'til they're gone, pan for gold 'til it's gone, then onto the next – always looking for the next thing – if you don't you're finished! Here maybe they're looking for nothing. Is that the difference here in the faces – a resignation? Like this is the way it is, nothing you do will change anything, is that it? They've had revolution, they've had war and all you do is suffer the same, generation after generation. And is that why Valmy's guys in the bar were so hostile, they didn't want change, change was a threat. Well, sorry guys but that ain't the American way!

Finally they leave the long, straight, tree lined main road to drive through country lanes until they enter the grounds of a large château. What greets him when the carriage pulls up is equally as weird as any of his earlier encounters. A rather grand, grey-haired individual comes out to greet them. He or she is dressed as a man in smock and trousers, but the smock, confusingly, seems to be of velvet and embroidered on the shoulders. They are smoking a cigarette and there's a lioness walking by their side. Irwin, nervous of the huge cat as much as anything, hangs back. He quietens the horse, fearing that it maybe as spooked as he is. 'You sober down now… and pray he's had his dinner.'

They don't approach until the animal lies down and the Dunhams alight from the carriage. He rides closer to Charles who is himself hanging back as the Dunhams exchange greetings with their host. He leans down from the horse, 'Say Charlie, is that a woman?'

'Madame Rosa Bonheur. She has a special permit from the police.'

'For the lion?'

'To wear trousers.'

Eventually Carrie Dunham comes over to them. 'Can you imagine what an honour this is? When I was a child I had a Rosa Bonheur doll.'

'You had a doll of this lady?'

'Irwin, you are looking at the greatest animal painter alive today. Bring the horse and I'll introduce you - and Charles, you don't need to translate, Madame has been to England and met Queen Victoria. Her English is excellent.'

Irwin dismounts, looking at Charles with an air of disbelief. He puts him in the picture. 'Cornelius Vanderbilt paid fifty-five thousand dollars for her picture of the horse fair.'

'Fifty-five thousand dollars? For a picture? He could have had the horses for that! And what's with the lion?'

Before Charles can answer, Dunham summons them and presents Madame with his gift of the mustang. She looks the horse all over before she takes a draw on her cigarette, nods and thanks him. 'Most kind. Buffalo Bill, he give me a Red Indian…' Irwin's suddenly listening, *did he hear right?* She continues, 'Maintenant, with this horse, I paint a picture of the Wild West.' Irwin is trying to keep his mouth shut but… 'You've met Buffalo Bill Ma'am?' Dunham enlightens him, 'Everyone meets Madame if they are in Paris.'

'Bill Cody's in Paris?'

She looks at Irwin, 'You know him?'

'Know him? As it happens I… I do... I was with him Ma'am - at War Bonnet creek. When he killed Yellow Hand... *First scalp to Custer*!'

All eyes are now on Irwin. Charles looks a little surprised. Carrie is impressed. Rosa Bonheur takes yet another drag on her cigarette, 'He is a good man.'

'Common as an old shoe – I like him, a real gent.'

She nods, possibly not understanding and summons a stable-lad to take the mustang. She invites them in. Irwin insists on seeing the horse settled into his new home. He's a little angry with himself. After that first meeting with Ellwood, he'd realized he was one question away from being exposed for what he truly was. He vowed then that the best way forward was to take a lesson from the card table – keep your mouth shut and remain the man of mystery. It was totally against his nature and here he was opening his big mouth once again *'First scalp to Custer… ' How stupid! Did I sound common?* The problem was, people loved his stories, always had!

Once the mustang was happy to get his nose in the trough, Irwin tries to rejoin the others, losing himself in a building that reminds him of a castle in a kid's fairytale and this strange man-woman, they treated her like some sort of queen... The oddest thing was, that in an effort to keep quiet he hadn't even asked why they were coming all this way to see a *painter*. All is revealed when a young woman directs him to the studio. *Studio?* It was a very large high-ceilinged room with the biggest, most ornate fireplace Irwin had ever seen. On the walls were the biggest paintings he'd ever seen and there, on one of several easels, was the answer to his question – The woman was showing drawings of a horse that was identical to the one in the advert he'd been carrying in his pocket. Charles explains that Madame was commissioned by Mr. Dunham to paint the prize-winning stallion that he'd bought two years earlier. An engraving of that picture was then made and that was the basis of the advert that was in every post office in the West. 'So that's what this is all about?'

'It is indeed and in return for the gift of the mustang, Mr. Dunham will ask her to make a new painting of the best horse he will buy this year.'

Irwin nods as if it's no big deal.

There are other people in the room now and he watches as a photographer poses Madame and her guests, urging them to remain absolutely still while he takes their photo. Irwin is jealous, *a photograph!* – if only he could have his photograph taken and send it back home – *if they could see me now!*

Charles is finally in his element, admiring the many paintings finished and unfinished, conversing in French with a youngish woman who points out details on the canvas. When the Dunhams rejoin them Charles reverts to English, comparing Madame's paintings with the works of other painters that he is familiar with. 'I'd say more powerful than Landseer, more refined than Troyen…' He doesn't include Irwin in these conversations, but Carrie tries to, telling him that Madame was the first female artist ever to win the Légion d'Honeur, then lowering her voice; 'I adore women that break out, defy convention – so brave! And yet she's accepted! She was telling us that she was so highly regarded at court that when the Prussians invaded, overran the country, destroyed everything in their path, the emperor ordered that her château, her paintings and her animals were all to be left untouched. The Empress Eugénie herself came here…' and the accolades keep coming, leaving Irwin feeling like he's stepped into another world, one in which he can make no contribution. It's very odd and isolating when people become so passionate about a subject that leaves you cold. He'd not done school, his mother taught him everything he needed to know. He had been a quick study, found reading and writing no problem at all, it had served him well. He'd never felt ignorant in his life – until now.

Madame takes them round the grounds, passing all sorts of animals, some in cages, some, like the lioness, walking beside her. She shows them her aviary, with all manner of exotic birds. Charles is aware that Irwin is uncharacteristically quiet and starting to hang back. He asks him if he is alright. He can only nod. 'I'm fine.'

'So you see what you're up against.'

'*Up against?*'

'It's a most sophisticated operation these days'

'You mean this is how they trade horses?'

'The lengths they go to.'

'You trying to tell me I ain't got a chance?'

'No, no.'

'You are Charlie, I can read your mind.'

'No...'

'You want to tell me how knowing about horses ain't enough anymore.'

'Not at all…' They walk on, Charles considering how to be diplomatic. '… but it is important that you know the odds, then if you work within your means...'

'Don't talk to me like a bankman!'

'I am so sorry.'

Carrie, hearing the tone of Irwin's voice, turns to look.

'You hear that? The bank man's trying to put me off my business.'

'Don't listen. If Cornelius Vanderbilt had listened to his bank I'm sure he'd have ended up working the railroads not owning them.'

'That's right! That's right! Thank you Ma'am! Did you hear that Charlie?'

The words of encouragement are all Irwin needs to regain his confidence. *She likes me!* While Dunham is taken up discussing technical matters with their host, Carrie walks with the two young men and it's not escaped Irwin's notice that she's always smiling when she looks at him… and she looks him in the eye… how inviting is that? Now's the chance to explain himself, but what version of himself should he tell? It seems that Charles has remained discreet and the story of the fire now feels a little far-fetched. He starts with the truth, the family history is always a good one; 'My grandpa arrived in Ohio with nothing. My pa, he went out to California with nothing. People said he was stupid, but you know what Ma'am? He proved 'em all wrong.'

'And so will you. I don't doubt it for a moment.'

'Why thank you!'

He glances again at Charles *you see?* Then he continues with the story of each new generation of his family knowing they have to change with the times – and that's what he's aiming to do now – even if it means son going against father and risking everything they've got and he admits that his funds are nothing compared to the likes of Ellwood, 'But if you have the knowledge and you have a dream…'

They are now heading back into the house and Dunham is waiting at the door for them. Carrie touches Irwin's arm 'Everyone needs a dream. You stick with us, my husband knows the men that matter and I'm sure he'll help you wherever he can.'

She takes her husband's arm and they go in. Irwin smiles at Charles who looks down, as though he's had his nose put out. Irwin puts his arm round him, he's a good, kind soul but so naive. He feels him tense up. He doesn't let him go.

He can't help but feel on top of the world when, two days later, he is in an open carriage with Dunham and Charles. Carrie, the children and their young governess are in the carriage behind. Irwin knows he owes this good fortune to Carrie. She clearly holds some sort of sway over her husband. The two men can talk horses all day long – the reasons why various of the draft horse breeds lack the Percheron's suitability for ploughing; the Shire horse's skirted feet clogging with mud, the Belgian's lack of wind and so on, but he still wasn't sure what this major player thought of him; would he really have invited him to the farm of the world's leading breeder of Norman horses if it wasn't for his wife? When there's a lull in conversation Irwin compensates knowing that somewhere in any silence there lies a truth, a conversation, he wants to avoid. Keep talking! Better to use the ride to show off his knowledge – to educate Charles in the ways of the horse-trading world. 'First rule in this business Charlie, is you don't trust no-one!'

Dunham interjects, 'I would suggest trust is vital.'

'Trust is absolutely vital Mr. Dunham sir, you are right... but when it comes to the tricks of the trade... We all know how low folks will stoop; you want to make an old horse look younger, you blow air under the skin…'

Charles looks horrified, 'You what?'

'You want to make him carry his tail high, you just stick a piece of ginger where you and I would not like to be holding a piece of ginger…' Irwin loves the look on Charles's face, '… ain't that right Mr. Dunham?'

'Of course you do have to be vigilant and that is why over the years we have built relationships that are based totally on trust.'

'That's what you have to do, that's what you have to do.' And Irwin pauses, worried that he might sound like one of the traders he's describing. He tries to think of a more edifying anecdote but he can't.

Soon the carriage turns off the road and passes through an archway revealing an imposing stone built farmhouse on one side of a quadrangle with stables making up the other sides. Peacocks wander round and sit on the rooftops, lending an air of the exotic. Irwin is impressed, 'Hell's oats!'

Monsieur Perriot, the stocky, mustachioed man who had welcomed the Dunhams to the banquet, comes out to greet them. They are taken inside, where the walls are adorned with large tapestries of rural scenes. Charles is kept busy translating as Perriot shows off his latest artworks. This is clearly a man whose star is on the up. Irwin is impressed, he's never seen a farmhouse like it, but he also can't help noticing that the Dunham's governess, who he's standing close to for the first time, is a wonderful shape. The soft roundness of her face seems to be echoed in the rounded curves of her breasts. She's holding the little girl's hand and smiles as she catches Irwin looking at her. 'I don't think we was introduced, I'm Irwin'

'Virginia'

And he leaves it at that as Wirth tugs at her arm desperate for a pee-pee.

After being offered aperitifs they move outside to the stables. Dunham has explained that as a stallioner, Perriot only deals in males, and has first call on all colts sired by his stallions. In that way he has the pick of the best breeding stock in the whole of the Perche. That, to Irwin, sounds like he has the whole business sewn up and explains the grandeur of the buildings. As they enter the stable block he is left speechless. The stalls, each housing a magnificent animal, stretch the length of the building. There's an atmosphere of hushed reverence, with occasional contented exhalations coming from the inquisitive giants. Carrie sees the look on his face and holds back as her husband and Perriot continue down the line. Irwin can't get past the first horse. He strokes it, looking up into its eyes, feeling its breath on his face. It's a communion. Irwin humbled in the presence of such a huge, yet gentle being. Carrie speaks quietly, ' You are now looking at the most cossetted breeding machines in the world…' She points to a board fixed above the stall , ' Have you noticed, look - each has his own dietary requirements written above his stall.' He can only nod in wonder.

Following the walk down the line the party watch as the grooms parade a number of stallions round the yard. 'This is my dream Mrs. Dunham – all this, this is my dream. Why not?'

'Why not indeed?'

Then a huge shining black horse with plaited mane and tail is trotted out. On command he rears up on his hind legs in front of the guests. The children gasp. Perriot sees Irwin raise his arms in wonder. He smiles proudly and addresses him in French. Irwin grabs Charles, 'What's he saying Charlie?'

'I think he said that this horse fathered the magnificent 'Brilliant' – that's the name of the horse - that won the gold medal at Chicago.'

'You bet he did! Ain't he the one! That's the one Mr. Dunham sir, I know that, you know that and he knows that!'

He can see Carrie smiling at him – she always seems to be smiling at him, like he amuses her. He does. For her husband it's a serious business, not that he's ever been one to show emotion, so Irwin's exuberance she finds a tonic, a bright light in any male gathering. Normally such a look would be an invitation that Irwin would be quick to take advantage of, but once again here, he looks away, not holding her eye, it's a strange unnatural feeling; forbidden fruit? So frustrating to be in touching distance of so much beauty all around... confusing.

The party is moving indoors, she's on the arm of her husband now and Irwin's walking alone, feeling very much the outsider. It gets worse when he's sat next to Virginia and the children for lunch. He needs to be closer to Perriot, to be able to hear Charles translating. There is so much he needs to know. Instead he has the governess trying to make conversation, 'Have you been to France before?' 'Is this the first time you've eaten peacock?' 'Do you know what this is?' She's very sweet, aptly named and at this moment in time, a pain in the ass. Eventually as they arrive at what appears to be the fifth course of the meal, the man sitting next to Charles, who Irwin assumes to be the Head Groom and who doesn't speak any English, excuses himself and leaves the table. Irwin is quick to take his place and start grilling Charles about the business side. 'I need to know how much…'

'How much what?'

'What sort of money are we talking here?'

'For the horses? It's not that simple…'

'It, is, it is, it is… Let me tell you something, I learned from my pa, *you look for the best, get shot of the rest.* That's how you build a business, that's what people respect. And this here is the best!'

'That's right and any horse here, if he is in anyway champion material, he will not be sold until after the show.'

'I can't wait till then.'

'Monsieur Perriot can. He will wait, like Mr. Dunham, to see which one wins the medals.'

'Then I'll be up against everyone. I need to get in first.'

'Irwin... I have no wish to pry into your financial affairs, but…'

'Charlie, I got the cash…'

'Oh no...' Charles stops eating, raising a hand to his brow and looks like he is in pain.

'What's up, you sick? Was it the peacock?'

'No, it's not the peacock.... but... 'cash'? Irwin...' Charles continues confidentially, turning his head away from the hosts. '… I feel that it is only fair to tell you... however much cash you may have... such is the competition this year that I have, just now, before we sat down, been instructed by Mr. Dunham to offer M. Perriot an open cheque.'

'You what?'

' So determined is he to secure the medal winning horses at the sales.'

Charles takes another mouthful of his apple dessert before Irwin can muster a response. 'Don't go stringing me a line here Charlie…'

Charles is summoned to translate, abruptly ending the conversation. Irwin pushes back his chair, Carrie is now involved with the children, everyone is engaged with someone. He walks past his uneaten tart and once back in the courtyard he lights a cigar that he'd been offered the night before. When things are going well he forgets he's even wearing the vest, but now he can feel the sweat of it against his back. He'd assumed that the many strokes of luck that had got him to Nogent, to meet the Dunhams and Charles, who'd even provided him with a bed, it had made him certain that this was meant to be. He'd thanked his mother every night and a hundred times every day, then this! *An open cheque?* He had no idea how much his gold was worth. There was no way he was going to trust someone like Valmy – the one person he'd met who he knew would be only too happy to help. Somewhere in the back of his mind he was waiting for the right opportunity to arise with Charles the banker, but that would only be when it came to a deal over his chosen horse.

A tall, thin young woman, a maid or a skivvy of some sort hurries across the yard. The drawn features, the care-worn eyes evoke his own sister – the last reminder he needed at this moment, '*And you know where you can get them for ten dollars!*'

Mark Dunham rides home in the carriage with his wife, leaving Irwin on his own with Charles. Even that feels like a snub and Charles's efforts to be helpful rub salt in the wound. 'I can tell you that all the main dealers, including Mr. Ellwood, who I know through the bank, have special arrangements paying over several years.'

'Then what you're telling is, I'm no better off than if I'd gone to Chicago?'

'I'm not saying that at all!'

But that's what it felt like and the rest of the journey back passes without a word being spoken.

It was like a kick in the guts. It was not an unfamiliar feeling. It was the story of his life; for every high there followed an even bigger low. If he'd been at home Irwin would have sunk into days of darkness, of speaking to no one, of taking off on his horse, heading nowhere, of lying under the stars that were so close he could pick them from the sky. Somehow his own insignificance out there would be a balm, he'd be absorbed into something infinite and he'd know he had to wait and the wretchedness would slowly pass, he'd be emptied and free to start again. So far from home that was a luxury he could not afford. He would not drink himself into oblivion. His mother was watching him, his father was watching, he could see his sister's twisted smile as she reveled in his failure.

SEVEN

He allowed himself one wretched, sleepless night; the hopelessness a wall reaching from earth to sky, until in a rage he kicked right through it. He is in the yard at dawn. The stable boys are already at work. He goes in and watches them carrying out the feeding and grooming. The animals are not all large and most of them are dapple-greys, one mare is even white. He tries to ask with the help of sign language where he can find himself a horse for the day. Unfortunately the boys answer him in French and talk amongst themselves meaning he doesn't understand a word. A female voice makes him turn. Jacqueline is standing in the doorway. 'Why you want a horse?'

'You! Thank God! I can't make 'em understand!'

She had heard his voice as she crossed the yard. He tries to explain. 'I need to get around. I need to find me a good stallion. To do a trade.'

'I see you with Monsieur Valmy yes? The other night? You go with him, no?'

'Valmy? No, no, no… He's a commission man, shifty as a mud bank - they play both sides against the middle, that ain't no good to me.'

She's not sure she understands, 'And Monsieur Dunham, you go with him, yes? I see you…'

Irwin sighs, 'Dunham, Ellwood… '

Jacqueline is called and turns to go. Her friend Sidonie is looking for her. He follows and stops her, determined not to let the opportunity pass. 'Ma'am… can I explain? I'm in a bind. I came here for a level playing field, if I'd known these guys have the whole thing sewn up… Dunham, Perriot…'

'Perriot? Why you go to Perriot? You Americans are not so clever you know?'

'You seen his stallions?'

'Oui, oui – and you spend so much money to buy the 'biggest stallion in the world.''

'You seen the size of the prairie? We need 'em big.'

'What good is the stallion without the very good mare?'

'Mares?'

'Mares not so much money.'

A man is calling her from the kitchen. She ignores him. 'My uncle he has the best mares.'

'One stallion and I can cover a hundred mares. I don't want mares…' He speaks to her confidentially as though the whole place is set against him. ' I need to know where I can find me a stallion that *Perriot* don't have no hold on... There must be someone out there…'

Jacqueline studies him, 'Oui, oui… I know man who…'

'You can help me?'

'No, no. He never sell to American. Not everyone like you, you know?'

'Oh come on, let me talk to the guy. I'm not buying hundreds of horses, I'm not Dunham. Say you come with me, explain?'

She looks to her friend who is now standing beside her, trying to follow the conversation. Irwin waits for her answer. She tries not to appear surprised.

'You want *me* to go with *you*?'

'If you would be so kind.'

'To tell you what is a good horse?'

'Oh no - I know a good horse.'

Jacqueline is now enjoying herself. 'No, no monsieur, you Americans you don't know.'

'I think we do.'

'Then why you have to come back every year?'

'We can't get enough of 'em.'

'No - you can't breed them.'

'Oh... oh, is that right…?' Somehow she knows a lot this girl. Dunham had told Irwin of his own problems with mares that were in too high a condition – producing fewer foals and many abortions. Irwin can only concede the point. 'All right - some folks they can't do it - they pamper 'em - we come from the land of plenty remember? But I ain't some folks and we ain't all that stupid...'

'Then you don't need me.'

'You can translate for me.'

'What is the point of that?'

He starts to lose patience. 'You know this place! You know the people - I need to find the best stallions and then...'

'Pourquoi? Why? Why look at something you cannot afford?'

'I beg your pardon Ma'am? I can afford… Believe me I got money – real money!'

'Then why you only got one suit?'

With that she turns and goes into the kitchen. Irwin paces the yard dumbfounded. *Is that what everyone thinks?* It's his best suit, it doesn't look too bad, it's not fancy like some of the Americans are wearing – one even prances around in some loud check patterned outfit. *How dare she!* In minutes Jacqueline reappears and Irwin is on to her. 'Who says I only have one suit?'

'Why you not put your clothes out to wash – laundry, yes? Like your friend, like others? And shoes? No shoes to clean?' She points to his uncleaned boots. He's now sure she's been in his room, maybe she rumbled him that very first night at the banquet… and she's not done yet.

'I tell you something Mr. Gurd - I think I have more dollar than you.'

'I don't think you do.' He wants to be outraged – she's a kitchen maid, he's a guest and she's looking at him in some superior, straight in the eye, kind of... Now she's putting her hand down her cleavage, *what the hell?* She produces a purse. She opens it up and shows him that it is full of paper American dollars.

'Voilà! Can you do that?'

Irwin is silenced for a moment. He puts his hand down his shirt – nothing happens. Jacqueline smiles, then Irwin flicks his fingers and conjures a gold coin out of the air, then another. It is Jacqueline's turn to be lost for words. 'Can you do that? Gold Double Eagles. You don't judge a book by its cover Ma'am.' Now it's his turn to smile. 'Will you come with me tomorrow? Take me to this guy you know, with the stallions?'

The game is over. Jacqueline's boss is calling her from the kitchen. She curses quietly to herself, putting the purse back down her dress, 'You really want me to lose my work here, don't you?'

'Of course not.'

'I'm sorry. It is too important to me.'

She turns to go but he holds her arm, 'And you don't know

how important this is to me!'

She shakes herself free. 'I can't help you.'

He watches her go in as her boss shouts for her yet again.

A groom comes out of the stables and calls, 'Monsieur…'

Irwin turns to see the lad leading a reluctant looking horse with a long straggly mane. He offers Irwin the reins, 'You want horse?'

The initial surprise that he had, after all, been understood, is tempered by the inability to find out why they were offering him this particular beast. The lads smirking between themselves and the horse's reluctance to move was not encouraging. Her name appeared to be Blanche and she was a sort of dirty white. Irwin was used to every sort of kicker and stubborn critter and after a good look over the mare, he accepts their offer and has her out of the yard and trotting down the street. He hadn't got a clue where he was heading, but by the time they reached the lower part of town, down by the river, he felt horse and rider were starting to know each other. He kicks her on only for her to prick up her ears, stop on the spot and rear up, enough to unsaddle a lesser rider. Irwin calms her down and sees the problem – they are right by a tramline – a line, that however much he tries, she will not cross. At some point the poor horse must have been badly spooked and now, when he listens, Irwin can hear the puffing of a steam locomotive, then the whistle and the poor horse rears up again and tries to turn and flee. He lets her have her head for a short distance, then pulls her up. Looking back he can see a funny little engine unlike anything he's seen back home. It pulls four little carriages on thin little rails. It makes him smile, the neatness of the thing, but the noise, the smoke and the smell clearly spook his ride. Is that why the lads were smirking? He'll have to find another way out of town.

He's surprised by the number of factories and mills along the river, but once he's beyond them he's into farmland. The horse takes him along lanes and ancient tracks bordered by small fields, orchards and forests. He soon finds horses grazing. He tries questioning men and women working in the fields and starts to recognize the words 'Monsieur Tacheau' and sometimes 'Perriot'. They all seem to shake their heads as they say it. Direct dealing clearly wasn't the way they did business. He does find one beautiful looking young stallion in a meadow next to an ancient looking cottage. He can hear babies crying so looks in through the open window. He would have looked away but is too surprised – a woman is breast feeding an infant. She was surrounded by half a dozen baskets containing babies in a standing position, the basket supporting them up to their armpits; so many little crying heads. It's the weirdest thing he's ever seen. For a moment he quite forgets the question he wants to ask. In the event he and the wet-nurse fail to understand a word the other says. He thanks her – mainly for not being in the slightest bit embarrassed by his intrusion and after that he thinks it is time to give up. It hasn't been a successful day. Riding back he comes to realise how much he needs a Valmy or a Jacqueline. Jacqueline… where did she get those dollars? Where did she learn English? He found the language here incomprehensible. How had she done it? He was impressed and intrigued.

Back in the yard the stable lads laugh when he manages to communicate the problem by the railway – they understand 'train' and are much amused that he has discovered the horse's weakness. They assure him the horse will never ever cross a tramline – '*jamais, jamais*!' The joke was on him.

He sees the Dunham children come out followed by Carrie and Virginia. It's been a bad day and he doesn't want to see them but he's stuck. Carrie waits for him to come over. 'We missed you today. We were expecting you to come with us.'

Irwin shrugs, not sure what to say.

'Are you going to the fair?'

He didn't know there was a fair, but before he can answer the kids are at his feet; 'We're going to see an Indian.'

'D'you want to see a Sioux warrior?'

Irwin has a sudden reaction against the whole family in their fancy clothes that shout of success. These people who have it so easy... He tries to remain polite and continue into the hotel.

'Thank you kindly, but I've seen all the Sioux I ever want to see… Killed me some too.'

Little Belle looks aghast, 'You did?'

'I had a little dog could smell 'em coming at five miles distance, so I was ready for 'em every time!'

He 'shoots' the kids a little too aggressively. He catches Carrie's eye as he goes to leave.

'Are you alright Mr. Gurd?'

He looks at her then goes inside. What is it with these moods? Where did that come from? He has to control himself.

He goes up to his room and finds a note pushed under his door. His heart sinks even lower. He didn't know and didn't like to ask Charles how long the room had been paid for. He assumed it was until the other boatload of guests arrived. Then what? Was this his marching orders? With some trepidation he opens the slip of paper stamped with the hotel's crest. All that's written is a name, 'Monsieur Caillard.' He studies both sides of the paper. It doesn't take long for Irwin to grasp at the hope that this has to be the man Jacqueline mentioned – the one he asked her to take him to. *It has to be him!*

He looks around the hotel and hangs about by the kitchen door, but he can't see her or her friend. The only person he sees is her unpleasant little boss-man. Instinct tells him not to ask him anything in case it makes trouble for her. He hears other guests talking about the fair, it sounds like the place to be – maybe she's there or maybe he can find Valmy? Maybe he'll know this man Caillard?

After washing, shaving, consciously smartening himself up as best he can, Irwin heads out and only has to follow the sound of a band playing to find his way to the fair. He is impressed, this place sure knows how to have fun! The musicians are a random group of guys playing mainly brass instruments with percussion and squeezebox. The trombonists in particular look like they are having a ball. The town square is packed with stalls and the whole town seems to have turned out. There's a big poster listing the attractions – top of the bill appears to be 'Le Dentiste' and the kids were right – there's a picture and a whole load of writing about 'L'Sioux'. Irwin wanders through the crowds and the stalls selling everything from cheese to wine to clothing and there's a whole pig roasting on a spit. It makes him realise he's starving, but then he sees a tepee. There's an Indian in full headdress sitting outside surrounded by a crowd. People seem to be paying to have their photograph taken with him. Irwin moves closer, the Indian is staring straight ahead, his face set like a mask. The sign next to him mentions Buffalo Bill's Wild West Show and Paris. Charles's words at the Bonheur woman's place echo in Irwin's head, *'It's a very sophisticated operation these days.'* Advertising – that's all this poor man was, a piece of advertising… He won't let himself be one of the crowd standing staring. He moves away to the bars that line the square. He can spot the Americans and the farmers in their smocks, but there's also a great assortment of other characters and some already, by the sound of their raised voices, look like they've been drinking for some time. He buys a pitcher of wine and sits watching, *surely Valmy will be here somewhere?* The smoke and smell of the hog-roast force him to buy a meal. Luckily it only takes a few of his francs. He tries to work out the money but gives up – everything seems to be very cheap. He sees various people from the hotel – guests and staff. Jacqueline's comments about his clothes have made him self-conscious; he turns away when he sees Carrie and the kids passing close by. Moments later he is forced to look when he hears a strangulated scream coming from one of the tents – 'Le Dentiste.' So it wasn't an act – it was the real thing! A man he recognizes comes out of the back of the tent – it's one of the hostile farmers he'd met that night with Valmy. The odds are that he could know Caillard if they both hate Americans, but he thinks better of asking him. Then he sees him – Valmy is limping along talking with a flashily dressed, got-to-be-American couple. He has to make a move.

He wanders over and puts out his hand. Valmy sticks his cigar in his mouth and shakes, 'Mr?'

'Gurd, Irwin Gurd…'

'I know, I know… Do you know Mr. Quinn?'

The man in the strange attire, with check trousers tucked in socks just below his knees, turns and Irwin instantly recalls the encounter in the bar with this man pinned to the floor by brother Jed. 'No… I don't believe we've met… Mr. Quinn…' He shakes his hand and relaxes when the man appears not to recognize him. It's a weird feeling – this man is the reason he's here. He rode away from home to hook up with this man and yet now face to face it's a whole different reality. What was he thinking? 'Have you just arrived?'

'I came over on the Normandie but my wife insisted we went to Paris.'

'Of course! Nice to meet you Ma'am – Irwin Gurd.' He swallows the last words, hoping they don't spark the man's memory. She nods but says nothing. She's younger than Quinn, that is to say late twenties, early thirties. Her attempt at a polite smile would also serve to say 'What is that smell?' He's ugly so she's obviously married him for his money, but which of them chose the flashy gear? He'd seen similar vulgarity once in the brothels of Kansas City, which looks like the sort of place they probably met. He's forced to continue the small talk learning that the couple are also staying at the Dauphin, but he is desperate to move on before Quinn recalls their earlier meeting. Luckily Mrs. Quinn is exhausted from the travelling and after arranging a meeting the following day with Valmy, the couple depart. Irwin wastes no time and produces his piece of paper. He asks Valmy if he knows this man Caillard. He does and confirms that he has stallions, Jacqueline was right. However she was also right about his hostility to Americans. Irwin begs Valmy to tell him where he can find him – if he can talk to him – he's not like the big guys, he only wants one horse. Valmy continues to dismiss the idea but Irwin takes him to the bar insisting that he is now happy to work with him as broker. When Valmy starts to talk about money Irwin reminds him who he was sitting next to at the banquet when Valmy first saw him; 'That young man, his name is Charles, he's a banker, his father owns the bank! I can do cheque, I can do cash, he's my friend, I can do anything!' Irwin has surprised himself here – he has yet to have certain conversations with Charles so the chicken is coming before the egg, but fortune favours the brave.... Nothing ventured nothing gained...

A short time later he is watching Valmy talking to a man sitting inside one of the other bars. Irwin has been told to stay outside and he can see why – he recognizes the same hostile crowd who'd been so abusive when he'd met them before. Valmy comes out insisting he should be very grateful, the man was very difficult to persuade, 'But I said you are not like the others...'

'That's right, that's right, I am not.'

'He will meet you, not here, but tomorrow at his farm, you can look and he can look at you.'

Valmy is happy to accept more drinks from Irwin as he explains how lucky it was that he had come to him. He knows these people and he knows that deep down, whatever they say, they would love some of those American dollars. The farmers here are poor and struggle to compete on their ever smaller plots of land which, since the revolution, had had to be divided equally between siblings every time a parent died. On top of that this is not the best land for grain, but what can they do? They can't all breed horses and Irwin has already learned how the stallioners control the market. The government's free trade deal with America was a useful scapegoat for those who haven't gone to work in the factories and who try to exist on the land they love. It's given the locals a reputation for being mean-spirited and sly, but Valmy understands them. He will make sure Irwin makes a good trade. When the conversation turns to money Irwin conveniently finds that he has to go. He had seen Charles and that's the perfect excuse. 'Don't you worry about the money – I'll go talk to my bank man!' And that is what he knows he must do.

He can feel alcohol in the air now, it feeds the great release, like the whole town is breathing out, letting go. Charles seems to have been given the night off by the Dunhams and is standing with other Americans watching a stilt-walker juggling. As Irwin approaches an argument breaks out when a drunken local farmer, confronts one of the visitors. All Irwin hears is 'Don't you push me!'. Abuse is hurled in both languages and in moments, the unsteady local seems to have fallen or been pushed to the floor triggering an all-out brawl. The stilt-walker goes flying along with his balls. Charles tries his best French to assist the man back to his feet only to be caught by the back of a Frenchman's fist and sent flying. Irwin is straight in there, grabbing the local and throwing him away from the fight – into a cheese stall. He turns back to see someone aiming a kick at the floored Charles. A right hook sends the man careering back into the mêlée as gendarmes' whistles blow and the law arrives. Irwin knows to take Charles by the arm and melt back into the crowd, as everyone starts protesting to the gendarmes, each blaming the other. Then a booming voice right behind them makes them turn, only to be confronted by a huge guy brandishing a gun in their faces. He is shouting at the top of his voice in French. He waves the gun around, aiming it haphazardly at people before trying to thrust it into Charles's hand, like he's pleading with him. Charles, terrified, is shouting back in French, until one of the gendarmes cracks the man on the head with his truncheon and he slumps to the floor. The giant's antics have upstaged the fight and all attention is now on him as he sits dazed on the ground holding his head while they retrieve the gun and handcuff him. It had all happened so fast, erupted out of nowhere.

'What the hell?' What was that about Charlie?'

Charles is in deep shock. 'He... he wanted me, he wanted me to... to kill him. He said he didn't want to live another moment in a country where they build monstrosities like la tour Eiffel.'

'The what?'

'The new tower... at the exhibition... Paris...I tried to explain to him that it was only temporary.'

'I tried to explain to him...' Irwin laughs, 'What world are you from Charlie?' He is now fired up with the adrenalin of the fight. He looks around almost like he's looking for more trouble, but drunken men are shaking hands, the stilt-walker is being helped back up to his full height and the cheese stall is being rebuilt. Anger is smoldering, but the party goes on. 'Crazy,

crazy… Don't you love this place?'

'No.'

'Oh come on - ain't you never seen a gun before?'

'Not aimed at my brain!'

Irwin laughs even more and tries to guide his white-faced friend towards a bar. 'Let me buy you a drink.'

'A *drink*?'

It's as though Irwin has said something truly disgusting.

'I am never drinking again! Can't you see what happens?'

'I want to talk to you Charlie…'

'What about?'

No answer - Irwin has seen Jacqueline dancing to the band with other young people. Charles repeats the question, but Irwin is already heading towards the performing area where earlier he'd seen a boring choir singing. The Dunham family are there, watching the band who had casually kept playing as the fight blew up. All thoughts of talking to Charles are now forgotten. He says 'hello' to all the family and tells them they should keep an eye on their young banker – he'd come close to shooting someone. While Charles tries to explain himself, Irwin watches Jacqueline dancing. She comes close to where they're standing, he calls to her, 'Jacqueline,' She pauses for a moment, 'I owe you Ma'am! A big thank you!' She shakes her head as though she doesn't know what he's talking about, then rejoins the dance. He watches knowing that she's keeping one eye on him even as she pretends to ignore him. Little Belle is doing her own dance and he goes under the rope and starts dancing with her. Virginia joins in with Wirth and they all do their own little country dance. He can sense that Carrie is watching him and would like to join them. He calls her to come under the rope, but she smiles and declines. He starts to dance with Virginia as the kids form their own dancing pair. Carrie watches Virginia looking into Irwin's eyes really enjoying letting her hair down. The music stops. Carrie catches Irwin's eye, indicates Virginia and mouths '*No!*' Irwin raises his arms, *As if I would!* He comes over to the rope and apologises for his sharpness with the kids when they'd met at the hotel earlier. 'Forgive me – I was having a bad day.'

'That's what happens when you don't come out with us.'

They're looking into each other's eyes now. He senses a game being played and with a drink or two inside him, he likes it. 'You sure you don't want to dance?'

She shakes her head. They both know she'd love to, but decorum dictates otherwise. Unspoken rules govern so much. They watch the dancing, each on a different side of the rope. Jacqueline comes spinning past. She grabs his hand and suddenly he's in the dance. So much for the rules now – so this is what happens when guests come under the rope – they get nabbed by the maid! He's piqued that she had the gall – would she dare do it to any other guest? She's spinning him round, then he's spinning her even faster; no pretending now! No airs and graces, finally he's himself, doing what he was born to do. He flashes past Carrie in a second, long enough to see she's watching him but the smile has gone – was it sadness he glimpsed or longing? No matter, the dance goes on and next time he looks the family have left.

Carrie wasn't the only one watching Irwin dance. A group of lads had been sitting eyeing up the girls. At the end of the evening when the dancing stops and the firework display begins, one of the lads, a young boy called Jean is taking a very keen interest in Jacqueline as she remains with Irwin, wiping sweat from his brow and playing with the buttons of his jacket. The lad is momentarily distracted by a rocket bursting overhead and when he looks back the couple aren't there. The main square is well lit by lamps but, much as he looks, he can't see them anywhere. Beyond the square it's moonlight and shadows, where have they gone?

There's lamplight along the main street of the town but Jacqueline has chosen to lead Irwin down a track away from the revelers who are now beginning to head to their beds. He doesn't ask her where they're going but once away from the hubbub he thanks her for the note she pushed under his door, now telling her that he is going to meet the man in the morning. She claims once again not to know what he's talking about. He stops and pulls her to him. He can see her eyes glinting, challenging, waiting… He kisses her. She doesn't resist. Her hands wander, finally opening a button on his jacket, slipping fingers inside. 'You are wet.'

'Ain't you? It ain't worth dancing if you don't end up wet.'

He knows what her game is and moves her hand. She laughs. 'It's hard – something in there… I feel…'

'No you don't.' He steps away, takes her hand and starts walking into the darkness. He changes the subject, 'You're from farming folk ain't you, like me?

'Folk?'

'Your family?'

'My parents, they are dead.'

'I sure am sorry to hear that.'

'Every year, Monsieur Dunham, Monsieur Ellwood, others too, they all give me dollars. I save them, you know why? I go to America.'

'Wow…' A big piece of the jigsaw drops into place. 'And that's why you learn the language?'

'How big is your farm?'

Irwin looks at her, expecting the next question to be 'You married?' But he loves her guts – this is his type of woman. They talk all the way down to the river. She knows about Ellwood and his special trains needed to carry all his horses. It's so absurd that Irwin only has to up the number of his own stock by a hundred to still sound impressive. He concentrates on telling her of what he's going to achieve once he's taken back a pure-bred Percheron stallion. Jacqueline wants to know everything about his life and the more he spins his yarns, as his farm starts to grow into something resembling a plantation owner's ranch, the more she is convinced, 'No one is poor in America.'

'What I say is, if you want something enough…'

He takes her face in his hands, for an age they try to read each other's eyes; eyes lit only by the moon. They let their lips find each other and there they stay. Eventually she leads him along a little path to a clearing on the river bank where they can sit hidden from the world. Nothing else is said, they both know enough of the other for now, of secrets hidden under shirts and in purses, even the river is silent, silent but powerful like the ocean; those thousands of miles that should lie between them. Strangely they have no desire to race across, kissing and caressing they want only to feel the power of the moment, the waves rising and falling, never breaking, surges coming from unfathomable depths while above, eyes-closed, they're touching stars, points of light in infinite darkness. They're up there at one with the heavens. If only time would let them stay. When finally they open their eyes and look up, the moon has crossed the sky. The sweat has gone cold on Irwin's back, the dew is on the grass. They get up and find themselves laughing, they both know the oddness of it – his jacket remains firmly buttoned and she had only felt his hand caressing the outside flesh of her thigh. It was a delicious difference, a deep intimacy that warmed them, had them smiling, repeatedly looking into each other's eyes all the way back to the hotel where they enter, quiet as mice, by the kitchen door. Irwin lies on his bed but has no desire to sleep. *What was going on? Was it the fact that she was French? That she didn't speak, she sang! Was that the difference?*

He is still awake when the bells of the goat-girl can be heard coming down the street. Irwin leaps up. Valmy is taking Quinn on a tour of stud farms, 'Haras' he called them. He had offered Irwin the chance to go along but he had decided to avoid Quinn for obvious reasons. The trip to Caillard's place has therefore been fitted in at the start of the day. He has a quick wash down. Looking in the mirror he remembers that his razor is getting too blunt for a shave and maybe Jacqueline could cut his hair?

They travel in Valmy's creaky old buggy, bouncing their way down ever narrower tracks, emerging out of woodlands at the head of a valley. Irwin instantly has misgivings; this is a million miles from the opulence of the Perriot place with its pristine stable blocks. The farm buildings here are ancient and there are signs that they've seen better days, with patched up roofs and one barn that's collapsed completely. How can anything this man produces compete? Valmy assures him, appearance is nothing – he must wait until he sees the goods! He goes off to talk to

Caillard who has seen them arrive but not stopped forking muck into a pile. In his brown smock and clogs he merges perfectly into the landscape, as timeless as the place itself. The two men talk but Caillard hardly even looks at Irwin before heading inside the barn. Meanwhile the mare in the adjacent paddock has wandered up to say hello. Irwin takes a closer look while he's waiting. It's a good looking animal but not groomed in any fancy way like he'd seen at the Perriot place. Valmy joins him. 'Old Caillard loves his horses, they're his life. You will be very lucky if he lets one go to someone like you.'

'We'll see.'

And they watch as a young, grey stallion is led out from the stables, there's a call from the mare, a greeting passes between the two horses.

A few words are exchanged between the two Frenchmen as Irwin examines the horse. Valmy comes up to him. 'It's a very fine horse, yes?

'Ask him who's the dam. Who is the mother of this horse?'

He asks the question and Caillard points to the mare in the paddock, a fact Irwin had already deduced. Valmy reassures Irwin, 'That's a very fine mare!'

'Very fine…' He points to the stallion. 'And he could be lame time I got him home.'

Valmy protests, insisting that this man's horses are as good as any in the Perche. 'What are you talking about, 'lame'?'

'Sidebones – if he ain't got 'em now, he will have. Always look to the mother Mr. Valmy sir.' He goes to the mare and points to the feet. He looks to Caillard and waves his finger. 'He knows, if he knows anything about horses, he knows. Now will you tell the gentleman that I ain't come here for his wind-broke old nags or cast-offs. One decent stallion sir, one, just one where this old girl ain't the mother.'

Irwin and Caillard stand staring at each other for some time, the latter almost smiling. Irwin asks Valmy to explain to the man that he is a simple farmer like him. He loves his horses just like he does and he's come thousands of miles to find the *one* horse that he can take home to save his dad's farm. He looks back to

Caillard and gestures; 'You and me, we're the same! We're not like the others and we live for our horses!' Valmy translates. The two men talk and Caillard walks off. Irwin asks what's happening. 'Is that it?'

'You are lucky man. He like you.'

'So?'

They wait and Caillard leads another full grown stallion out of the barn. This one has strong, powerful hind quarters and a massive neck. Valmy claps Irwin on the shoulder and utters a string of superlatives, 'Superbe! C'est magnifique, n'est pas? Le meilleur dans le Perche!' Typical broker talk – fine words mean nothing. Irwin looks it over as Caillard fetches the dam. Every feature of both animals is scrutinized in great detail with Caillard studying Irwin as intently as he is studying the horses. In the end Irwin turns and nods to the two men. He shows no emotion – the deal has still to be done, but deep down he is screaming, *Yes!!*

Impatient as he is to complete the purchase, he accepts that Caillard is intent on showing the horse at the sales. If it wins an award it will affect the price, but Irwin is assured that he is the only American he will sell to. In reality it's a stroke of luck as he has no way to pay until he has sorted out the gold. They shake on the deal in the same way that Irwin has shaken on deals back home – going on instinct, only going with those you trust and for whatever reason these two men have decided to trust each other.

On the way back Valmy is in a very good mood. So - Caillard is selling his best horse, one that has a reputation throughout the Perche. The lure of the Yanky dollar has finally got the better of him. Like Irwin, like Caillard, Valmy is an outsider and this will make him a player. For Irwin the pressure is now on. He spends the bone shaking journey weighing up his options. Maybe his early fantasy about hooking up with Quinn is now a possibility he has to consider? The cattleman's dress suggests he has stupid amounts of money. He'd be impressed by the pure gold. Without mentioning that he floats the idea to Valmy; that Quinn being a cattleman will have no idea what he's buying, but as Valmy can see, Irwin has the knowledge, if they teamed up… Valmy seems suspicious, wary of anyone encroaching on his clients. Irwin drops it for the moment and considers the other option of going to Charles. He remembers his reaction when he mentioned 'cash'. What the hell would he say to 'gold?' But that's not his biggest problem; what he's wearing, the gold laden vest that's weighed him down since he left home is something he's frightened of revealing, of letting go of, of changing into paper like some reverse alchemy. His pa had buried it deep in the earth for the same reason. Who can he now tell and trust? The flashy Quinn? Charles the banker? Or Jacqueline who is already on the scent? He desperately needs to know its value and it's now or never. As they arrive back in town he decides it will have to be Charles. Having resented banks for holding his family's future in their hands for years, he was going to have to put himself at the mercy of one of their kind once again. He can picture the horror on Charles's face as he shows him the vest. At least that will be a moment he can savour!

His mind is made up as they pass under the arch into the hotel yard. It is unusually crowded with people. Some he recognizes, including Quinn who he suspects is waiting to go off with Valmy, but others are not so familiar. As they pull up Irwin is aware that all eyes seem to turn their way. He now notices Charles and the Dunhams, Ellwood and the chief of police who had been so put out at the banquet. Why are they looking at him? Why have they all stopped their conversations?

Valmy is also suspicious, muttering under his breath like one who is always the victim. Irwin jumps down, 'So, how's it going? Hi Charlie!'

Charles steps forward, 'Irwin these gentlemen have something to ask you.'

'To ask me?'

It's Ellwood who poses the question, 'Where were you last night?'

'Last night? Me? At the fair.'

'And after the fair?'

'What is this? What's going on?'

The chief of police asks the young lad Jean, who had been so keenly watching Irwin and Jacqueline the night before, if this is the man he had seen. He nods. There's an exchange between the French speakers including Fournier, the hotel manager, Tacheau one of the farmers who had been at the top table at the banquet and the police chief. Irwin interrupts, 'What the hell is going on? Charlie, what's their problem?'

Ellwood is the one to answer. 'Someone's been doping horses.'

'What?'

'Two of Monsieur Tacheau's finest stallions.'

'Why you looking at me? Charlie, why they looking at me?'

Before he can answer Quinn steps forward, 'I got it! I knew I'd seen you before! Where's your brother country boy?'

'I ain't got a brother! What is this? Why would I dope horses? Why would I want to do that?'

And Quinn is there again, 'To bring down the price.'

'Why?'

'To make it closer to something your sort can afford.' And he turns to the others, 'I know this man!'

Now Irwin is getting mad, 'You don't know horse-shit! Charlie, you saw me – I was at the fair dancing with Jacqueline.'

'And after?'

'I was with Jacqueline.'

Ellwood moves closer, 'Doing what exactly?'

'I don't think that's no-one's business except mine and Jacqueline's.'

'It's everyone's business where you were last night.'

'Alright, we ain't got nothing to hide, ask her.'

'We have. She says she left you after the fireworks.'

That throws Irwin. He asks if he can speak to her only to be told that she doesn't work there anymore. She broke the rules. Employees are not supposed to mix socially with the guests. Her family have come and taken her back to their farm. Irwin raises his arms in the air, challenging the police chief to search him, search his room – how was he supposed to have done the doping, anyway - he didn't even know where Tacheau's farm was – it was all madness! He begs Charlie to back him up but he apologises; he is sorry to say that Irwin has to admit that he was very late coming back. He had himself had a sleepless night owing to terrible pains from where he'd been kicked in the fight. He had heard him come back to his room just before dawn. Irwin can't believe what's happening. Why is no one standing up for him? They are all stitching together a very convenient case; now Fournier is suggesting that that was why he needed to go off on his own with his own horse; 'L'Américain qui monte seul.' - *The American who rides alone*. The only one who speaks up for him is Carrie who asks what actual evidence they have against Irwin. Silence – they have none and that makes him lose his rag, railing at Ellwood in particular, who always seems to have doubted him. He confronts the police chief insisting that he search his room and... *Hell's teeth!* He goes cold at the thought that he had already begged them to search his body, *the vest!*. He turns and walks away, his own foolishness compounding his shock. He can hear Carrie arguing for him, but everything's a blur. It turns out they had already turned over his room. All the police chief can do is insist he reports to the gendarmerie the next day with his passport. Not easy - all he has are his signing-on papers for the voyage, he shouldn't even be here, but that's a problem for another day. He was so close...so close... now Charles, who he needs more than ever, won't even look him in the eye. As the crowd disperses Quinn has the last smug laugh; 'Looks like you've been playing out of your league country boy.'

An hour later Irwin is galloping cross-country with the youngest of the stable lads hanging on for grim-death behind him. They slow down when they come to a hamlet of half a dozen small cottages. There's one group of farm buildings set back off the lane. The lad points and Irwin dismounts, gives the lad a coin and asks him to wait. As he walks down the short track he is met by angry geese raising the alarm. Irwin is trying to work out if any of the barn-like buildings are inhabited when a woman appears in the doorway of one of them wiping her hands on a cloth. Irwin, held back by the angry gander, calls, 'Jacqueline? I need to see Jacqueline!' The woman, short, stocky, round-faced, which Irwin had come to recognise as the local breed, waves him away, not so much unfriendly as deeply hostile. A man, of similar mould, appears from another building. Irwin curses silently – he'd seen this guy before; he was one of the mob that had given him grief in the bar with Valmy. No wonder Jacqueline knew all about the hostility to Americans – her family were part of it. If the woman was in her forties then the man could be her son. Both seemed to have anger engrained in their features; was life that hard? It was a familiar look – he'd seen it with homesteaders, those brought down by false promises from land-agents; the look of those surviving without hope. Here he sensed he was walking into trouble. Why else had the man come out with a horsewhip? All he can do is ask calmly If he could please talk to Jacqueline. He understands 'Non Jacqueline!' and there was no mistaking the gestures. He can't leave without seeing her, she is his only hope. He holds his ground. Now the man is there the geese have at least shut up. It's a stand-off, with Irwin repeating that he has to see her and the mother and son shouting at each other. Eventually Irwin advances towards the house, 'Ma'am, understand this – I ain't going nowhere until…'

There's a shout from a barn, 'Go Irwin! '

He turns and makes out Jacqueline inside the building, framed in the open top of a stable doorway. He goes over, ignoring the shouts of the man. She retreats, 'Go away! You should not have come here!'

'I gotta a problem…'

'You got a problem? *You got a problem??* Go!'

He's now at the doorway and stops. As sunlight catches her in the gloom, he can see one side of her face is red, her eye bruised. He looks back at the man, standing whip in hand. 'Who did that?' He puts out a hand to her. She screams 'Eloigne toi de moi!!'

He takes a step back. 'Okay, okay… You're worried for fear ain't you?'

'You want to see me locked in convent?'

'Locked? I don't want.. No!'

'That's what they do – I see you they lock me in convent.'

'You said I wasn't with you last night.'

'And why you think I say that?'

The whip cracks behind him, the man is getting impatient. Irwin tries quietly one last time. 'Did they tell you what they was accusing me of? I just need you to tell 'em I was with you the whole of last night, that's all.'

She goes and throws herself on an old straw mattress and sobs. The whip cracks again, Irwin has to hold back, stopping himself from facing the man, *Oh that you was in my country, I'd whip your dirty ass...* He takes a breath, takes one step to the door and says under his breath, 'I'll be back.' He walks away. There's now another older man and the young boy Jean in the doorway with the woman. He spits as he passes, 'Is that where you keep her? Shame on y'all! Animals!'

It's a slow ride back. Slow enough for the lad to walk alongside, for the horse to grab leaves from the hedgerow and Irwin to do nothing to stop her. He is so upset by what he has witnessed. It has numbed him; she was fearless - the most spirited girl he'd ever met. What could make her so afraid; the whip? Fear of being locked away in a *convent*? What was this place? *Medieval* is that what they call it? It's what they called the castle on the hill high above the town. A shudder goes through his entire body, a feeling like even the horse is complicit, leading him through a very ancient land. There are flashes of panic, cut adrift from everything he thought he knew, he can feel the place engulfing him.

He's still reeling from the events of the day as he makes his way back up to his room, not having any idea what his next step will be. He can't work out what he has done to turn people against him. All he wanted to do was buy a horse...

He hears voices on the landing, it's Carrie and Charles talking in the doorway to Charles's room. He doesn't want to see them. But it's too late, Carrie is there barring the way to his room. 'Irwin, Charles has told me the sad circumstances which have brought you here...'

'He had no right to tell you nothing!'

'I'm sorry about your mother, such a terrible way to die. I don't know and I don't wish to know your circumstances but if there's anything we can do – I have told Charles he should help you anyway he can.'

'Well that's a fine job he's done so far!'

'You were with Jacqueline all night?'

'Is that a crime?'

He tries to get past them into his room. Carrie stops him and explains that it's the biggest crime he could commit – Jacqueline is an orphan, when her parents died she became the ward of her aunt and uncle and it was arranged that when she was twenty one she would marry her cousin and his family would then inherit her family's land. It was well known to everyone in the hotel that she was determined that wouldn't happen. Irwin calms down as the situation starts to make sense, 'Is that why they all want to get rid of me?' Carrie shakes her head. The likes of Quinn who claim to know him from before haven't helped and she's tried to talk to the locals, but her French is not that good. She suspects he's a scapegoat – an easy target, covering up something the locals don't want to talk about. She apologises to him, she's done what she can but the stakes appear to be very high for a whole lot of people. At that point she has to leave with Irwin questioning exactly what she means. He asks Charles; he speaks French; what's going on?

Charles can only repeat the warning that his father had given him before he left, 'He told me to beware; you will meet foreign women who will flatter to deceive.'

'What you talking about?'

'Desperate to get to America. Like Jacqueline, Irwin – she's nothing but a gold digger!'

He has to go into his room before he hits the guy. He drops down on the bed, the vest, the vest, it feels so heavy! And he can see his father, *No!* He sits up, pushing all family thoughts from his brain. He has to stay strong, but how? How can he talk to Charles now? Talk to Carrie? He has to pull himself together, remind himself that he has found a brilliant horse, that he now understands Jacqueline's dilemma. But *doping horses?* Where did that come from? And what of his compatriots – Ellwood and Dunham – why are they against him? He's talking now, voicing his thoughts out loud. 'Dunham knows me! I helped him! Yet he never opened his mouth...'

He has to eat, he'll go back to the fair, it's supposed to run all week. He can't stay in his room. He can't get the image of Jacqueline out of his mind, he'll sort something, he can't leave her there! He hurries down the stairs. He's going through the lobby and he sees Ellwood and Dunham in the lounge. Without thinking, he's in there. 'Gentlemen, I don't know what's going on, but come on – come on now gentlemen - you know I had nothing to do with this doping stuff.'

Ellwood takes his cigar from his mouth. 'Young man, I started on a dollar a day; do you know how much I am worth now?'

'No sir.'

'Neither do I – that's how much I am worth and if I had once tolerated individuals who jeopardised my interests, I would not be worth a cent.'

'And how have I done that?'

Dunham now speaks quietly, 'We have gone to great lengths to establish friendly working relations with these people...'

'So have I!'

Irwin's wry smile is a mistake. Ellwood is not amused, 'You think that's funny? This is not funny. You have done harm to our relations with these people.'

'And how have I done that? You truly think I doped the horses?'

'You have made yourself unwelcome Mr. Gurd.' Dunham still won't look at Irwin, 'We think you should reconsider your position here.'

Irwin wants to explode, *How dare they!* Charles walks in, sees Irwin and about-turns but not before Irwin stops him. The anger's boiling up now, 'Charlie! Charlie – you tell them, you know I was with Jacqueline – why else have they taken her away? Tell them! I could not have doped those horses...' Irwin waits,

Charles is extremely embarrassed but doesn't know what to say. 'You believe me don't you? Just say it!!'

'The Battle of War Bonnet Creek was in 1876.'

'So?'

'By my reckoning that would have made you about seven years old.'

'So?'

'You told Madame Bonheur that you were there, with Colonel Cody.'

'So?'

'I don't know what to believe anymore, I'm sorry. I'm sorry…' And he turns and goes. That has thrown Irwin for a moment. All he can do is thank the men for their support and leave the hotel.

At the fair he eats and drinks. It's raining so there is not the same crowd of people. The Sioux is sitting alone, it's possibly too wet for the photographer so there is no queue of people. Irwin sits watching him, feeling for the man and feeling an odd bond between them – outcasts… He wanders over. He tries to decipher the billboard alongside the tepee, but his attention is really on the bizarreness of the Indian's situation. The man is sitting motionless, staring into space, a pose he seems able to hold for hours. Irwin feels an urge to talk to him, to connect. He tries to remember bits of their language picked up in bars, and from squaws he had known… He moves closer, 'A long way from home, huh?'

'You stole my home.'

Irwin backs away *Where did that come from?* The man had not blinked, not moved his head, hardly moved his lips, but from somewhere deep down came that instant rebuke. So much for a bond, it's more like the man knew the way Irwin had been way back when... A young girl won in a game of cards… With a pang of guilt he heads for the bar. He'd mixed with many godless men, but his mother had brought him up with the Bible and for him there was no escape, guilt was a real thing. He desperately wanted to be forgiven for some of the things he'd done; when he'd gone along with the guys all in the name of having some fun. *Do unto others as you would have them do unto you.* He buys a pitcher of wine, then another, until he sees the stable lads from the hotel coming out to play as the sun sets. It gives him an idea. One more pitcher of wine and it will be dark…

The horse knows him now and doesn't seem to question a night time excursion, or to mind the rain. She even seems to know the way to the hamlet. She's not too happy once they find themselves down a wet, overgrown track as Irwin tries to skirt round to the back of the farm. He dismounts, ties up Blanche and makes his way across a small field towards the barn where he hopes to find Jacqueline. Much to his relief he makes it all the way to the door without a sound from the geese. It appears to be locked in some way. He taps lightly, whispers Jacqueline's name. He's looking for another way in when the door creeks. He whispers her name again. She silences him. More creaking sounds, the door opens a little way and very slowly she creeps out, her finger to her lips, 'My brother… he sleeps…'

She leads him away from the barn, whispering, 'What are you doing here?'

'You want to go to America?'

'You crazy!!'

'That's right. I ain't seeing you locked up in no convent!' He tries to hold her, she winces, pushing him back before he can kiss her. She looks around clearly scared. He tries to reassure her. 'I'm not messing around here, but I'm in as big trouble as you. I need you to come and swear on the Bible I was with you last night.'

'Gaston kill me!'

'No he won't 'cause you ain't going to be here – you do that for me, I can buy me that stallion and we can all go back together; you, me and horsey come too!'

She shakes her head, 'Non non… c'est impossible…'

'No - *possible*, I swear! I'm taking you with me! I promise you!! You believe me don't you? I can do it, look…' He taps his chest – 'You know I got a heart of gold!'

She puts her hand out to feel. He opens his jacket and his shirt, let's her slip her hand inside. She's now close to him, looking up into his eyes, trying to work out what's going on. He slips an arm round her waist, pulls her to him and they kiss. For a moment they're back as one, lost to the night, in a place where anything is possible, but not for long, the winds up now, driving squally rain and a door bangs. She starts, pushes back and they listen. It's nothing but it's turning into a rough night. He holds onto her, stopping her from backing towards the safety of the barn. 'Jacqueline - we got something you and me – something I ain't never had before… I beg you trust me Jacqueline – I will not let you be locked in no convent. Now I got the horse right over the pasture there…'

She throws herself at him, desperately wanting to trust him. They more they kiss the more she lets herself believe his promise. To be in this strong man's embrace is to be safe, to be free. She won't let him go.

They're deaf to everything but the wind and the creaking of timbers until a shower of thatch comes down with the rain and a body drops from the roof, flattening them both. Jacqueline screams, trapped under Irwin, then screams again as wood cracks down on his head. Only then does Gaston struggle to his feet. Then there's another body in the rain, a skirt wielding a shovel. Irwin looks up, turning to see it coming down on his back. He hears Jacqueline screaming as she is dragged away. Many voices now, shouting, the full weight of the woman pinning him down, his face is being pushed into the mud, another body across his legs, a sack is pulled over his head. He struggles to breathe, flashes of cattlemen wrangling steers, lying across them to brand 'em, castrate 'em, *God help me!*

EIGHT

It's not the first time Irwin's been locked in a cell, but nothing like this, this one is stone, stone-cold, damp like a hole in the ground, the only light coming from a grill high up by the ceiling. He has no idea how he came to be here and has the worst headache he's ever had in his life. He's tried shouting for help but it sends a pain right through his skull that sends the room spinning and has him sinking to the floor, sick as a dog. Flashbacks of headlocks, *can't breathe!* Pitch black night with hands clawing at his face… his mouth pulled apart… *choking…* Whatever the liquid was that they forced down his throat, he only remembers it burning, then nothing… Then he woke up here. He shivers, running his hands over his half-naked body, knowing, knowing, knowing he should be banging on the door, screaming *shouting…* he can't do it. He has to close his eyes, desperate for the room to stop spinning round.

*****

Jacqueline's young brother Jean brings a bowl of soup to the barn. He unties his sister, whose one wrist is roped to a pillar. She tells him she is bleeding and demands that he leaves her to clean herself up. He reluctantly agrees to give her five minutes while he feeds the pigs. As soon as he is gone she is off, out of the farmyard and across the field. Irwin's horse is still there, hidden behind the hedgerow on the overgrown track. By the time Jean returns to the barn she is on her way to town.

She knows this is her last throw of the dice. Going anywhere near the hotel is a massive risk but she also knows what her family are planning to do – by the end of the day they will have her in the convent. She has to take the risk. She makes it into the kitchen where her friend Sidonie tells her that Irwin is locked up at the gendarmerie, accused of horse doping. Fournier comes in. Jacqueline pushes past him, ignores calls for her to stop and hurries up the stairs to the bedrooms – the Americans are now her only hope. She bursts into Charles's room, part relieved, part surprised to see him sitting working at his desk. She's not as surprised as he is. Her clothes are mud-splattered and her face is bruised and filthy. 'You have to help me!'

Charles has never felt so far outside of his comfort zone. She's grabbing his arm, she's begging him, she swears to him that Irwin was with her all the night of the fair. If he will come with her she will go to the gendarmerie, or swear in front of a notaire – Irwin couldn't have doped any horses. He's innocent! She'll do whatever she has to do to help him. When Charles asks why, she tells of Irwin's promise to take her back to America. He feels obliged to disabuse her of the idea. 'You may not wish to hear this, but Mr. Gurd is not what he seems – I doubt he has the means to take you to Paris, let alone America.'

'He said…'

'He said a lot of things; his family burned in a fire apparently; true or false? I do not know, but I do know that some men live in a fantasy world, you know that word, 'Fantasy'?'

There's a knock on the door. It's Carrie's voice outside. Charles doesn't know what to do. He calls, 'One moment please…' He folds and locks his writing slope as Carrie tells him his services are required – the police are downstairs. He hears the door of the armoire click shut and turns round; Jacqueline's nowhere to be seen. He hesitates then leaves the room.

Carrie leads him down to the lounge where a number of people, including Dunham and Ellwood are waiting with the police chief. Charles is asked to translate. In so doing he learns that Irwin was found semi-naked in a ditch, senseless through drink. More important to the police chief was the fact that in his hand he had a bottle of chloroform; it was chloroform that was used on the plugs of cloth that were found stuck up the noses of the doped horses. This hard evidence and confirmation of Irwin's guilt causes much consternation amongst the Americans. When Carrie questions why anyone would do such a thing, Ellwood explains that it makes a good horse look out of condition and puts people off buying it. That one of their own would stoop so low is very embarrassing. The police chief meanwhile is increasingly agitated and gabbling in a way that has Charles struggling to translate. *This is not the French he was taught back home.* As far as he can make out the man wants to know what they intend to do. He has Irwin at the gendarmerie where he is screaming and creating hell, accusing the gendarmes of stealing his clothes. They need to know who he is before they can charge him but he has no papers. Dunham agrees that they will look for his papers in his room and then he will send Charles to sort everything out. Even as he then relays this information in French Charles is thinking, *Why Me??* But what can he say? Dunham and Ellwood have concluded that the best thing is for them to send Irwin back home immediately at any price and keep the whole sorry business out of the public eye. There's no lasting damage to the horses, so no one need ever know and their reputation as honest brokers will remain intact. That seems to pacify the police chief but just as he's preparing to leave Fournier comes up from the kitchens followed by Gaston. They're looking for Jacqueline, they know she's in the hotel, has anyone seen her? Charles makes the mistake of saying, 'Umm…' which has all eyes turning his way. What can he say? 'I think… I think she's in my wardrobe.' Even as Fournier and Gaston head up the stairs and the others remain staring at him, he knows that didn't sound quite right and it's something he will never adequately explain, but he does his best and is soon relieved to be out of the building and heading for the gendarmerie.

He has no idea what to expect when he finds the place. He has had to sort out some of his own clothes as he's been told Irwin is almost naked and he seems to have nothing in his room. His animosity towards his fellow countryman is growing by the minute as he locates the forbidding looking building and makes his way through the front door. It's not what he expected. There's what he deems to be a peasant woman waving a rabbit about and shouting at the gendarme behind the counter. She's pointing to a white patch of fur and as far as Charles can make out, she is claiming that this rabbit had an identical twin and the woman's brother has stolen it. It has the same white patch so the gendarme should take it as proof. She's trying to give it to him. She puts it on the counter at which point there's a desperate distant shout - Irwin yelling at the top of his voice. The rabbit jumps off the counter, much to the relief of the gendarme who can now turn his attention to Charles as the woman scrambles about on the floor trying to catch her precious lapin. Charles says a polite 'Bonjour,' and points in the direction of the still shouting Irwin. He is led through to the cells which stink of excrement. It's not quite as Charles had been led to understand. Irwin is now wearing his own jacket and trousers although they look wet, muddy and creased. When the door is opened he throws himself at Charles. There's a look of desperation in his eyes the like of which Charles has never seen – and the smell! 'The vest!! Charlie, they taken my vest!' It's some time before any semblance of calm is restored and they are led through to a small dark office. Irwin looks ill and can only keep protesting; 'Ask 'em about the vest!' This gendarme behind the desk is the form filler and wants details. Charles asks Irwin for his name.

'You know my name!'

'Irwin Gurd – is that your real name?'

'What are you talking about?'

'I'm sorry, I'm not enjoying this…'

'Hell's teeth – the vest!!'

'Your vest is the last thing…'

Irwin grabs Charles so violently by the lapels that the gendarme jumps to his feet.

'Charlie, I am going to tell this – every cent I have was sewn in that vest - gold Double Eagles – near two thousand dollars worth.'

There's a moment of complete silence. The gendarme resumes his seat.

'You really don't have a bank?'

'They've stolen everything I have. Ask him – have they got it?'

Charles can't think of the French for vest but does his best to demonstrate which only serves to add to the form-filler's belief that all foreigners are mad. He becomes increasingly demonstrative; clothes are not important, why ask about clothes? The most important thing in the world is for Irwin to have the correct papers – 'le passeport!' Irwin seizes the opportunity to blame everything on the robbers; as well as the gold, he claims all his papers were in the vest – they have to find the vest! He tries to give his account of the night before but keeps seeing and hearing Jacqueline. Trying not to involve her makes everything far too vague for the form-filler, too confusing for Charles and impossible for Irwin to explain why a chloroform bottle was in his hand. He feels his head spinning again and leaves the room in spite of the form-filler's protests. He collapses onto the nearest bench where he finds himself next to a mumbling woman with a rabbit.

Charles has to part with a sum of money before the bureaucracy is satisfied and he can assure the man that the embassy will sort out Irwin's papers and he will return.

There's an odd irony as the two young men make there way back through the town to the hotel; the same thought lurks in both their minds; *Why me?* Charles can smell Irwin even though they are now in the fresh air. The police had in fact recovered all his clothes from where they found him and his boots seemed to be smeared with manure of some kind. It feels like he's walking alongside the sort of hobo that once accosted him outside the railway station in Chicago. It's unbearable! He is overcome with the same emotion as when his parents had philanthropically employed a family of freed slaves and insisted one of their children went on a church outing with him. Then and now he was sure that everyone was looking at them. For Irwin it was the simple rage of the injustice of it all. He knew he'd done nothing wrong but just because of who he was, he was being framed for something he hadn't done. He felt like it had been that way all his life. The self-pity disappears in a flash as they reach the hotel and a mule comes galloping out through the archway pulling a small cart. Gaston is driving and sitting next to him, she's there...

'Jacqueline!'

'Irwin!'

Gaston cracks the whip and the mule races off down the street, Jacqueline looking back helplessly. The lovers remain staring until there's nothing left to see.

'I gotta do something…'

'There's nothing you can do.'

Charles tells Irwin that he must forget her. Jacqueline will be taken to the convent and there she will stay until she comes of age and she and her cousin are married. Irwin insists that it's barbaric and *'she ain't no nun!'* But Charles defends the local custom, 'She's not going to be a nun, it is simply to protect young women from the likes of….' He doesn't complete the sentence but the inference is all too clear. To rub it in he explains that young women are particularly vulnerable these days as they have seen stable lads who have accompanied horses across the sea and have written back with tales of great wealth. In Jacqueline's case she had come to Charles's room and he had tried to explain to her that where Irwin was concerned there was no such pot of gold at the end of the rainbow. Irwin is desperate to wipe the smirk from his face. 'You told her what?'

'I told her nothing but the truth.'

'And what truth was that?'

'That you were in no position to take her to Paris, let alone America…'

'You hired your pallbearers yet?'

'No.'

'Well I advise you do – cus by the time you die you ain't goin' to have a friend left in this world. There's more than one kinda truth.'

And he walks off into the hotel, not even sure where he's going or why he's even there anymore.

Fournier is the first to confront him, calling him back as he starts to go upstairs. Charles comes in and the two men talk in French. Irwin guesses that maybe he has lost the room. He waits, expecting the worst, expecting to be thrown out. He's ushered into the salon, where bit by bit the court of his fellow countrymen is assembling. Americans he has avoided ever since he arrived are there - major players, names like Dillon and Sanders, white haired, bewhiskered, solemn faced. He notes how big they appear as they seem to fill the room, much bigger than the locals and more finely dressed. Then Ellwood walks in, of course, and Dunham and finally the vulgar Quinn. He sees no reason why he should answer to them but what can he do? He wants to run away but where can he go? He notices Carrie coming down the stairs, their eyes meet for a moment but she doesn't come in. She looks appalled at the state of him. Is she deserting him too? He watches her go down towards the staff quarters, leaving him aware of his own filth. Dunham breaks the silence in the room by saying how disappointed he is in Irwin. He can't understand how someone who loves horses as he clearly does could then go to such lengths to harm them. What's the point of defending himself? It feels like he's being ambushed by the town vigilantes and the noose is already swung over the branch. His energy has gone, he shrugs and quietly asks why he would dope a horse he could buy? Quinn smirks, it's the funniest joke he's heard that day. 'Did you say, 'you could buy' country boy?' He recounts his earlier meeting with this penniless bar-brawler in Abilene. They all seem to agree that what he's done was the action of a desperate man. *I was not a desperate man!* He has to tell them about the vest, but knows even as he does so, how crazy it sounds and he knows that they won't believe him. Their minds are made up, He is well aware as he tells the tale of his father's Double Eagles that it sounds like his most far-fetched lie so far. He admits to his relationship with Jacqueline only to point out that it was her cousin who has to be the villain of the piece – he's the one who has the most to lose. If Jacqueline doesn't marry him then he will lose her land. 'He's set me up!' The simple sincerity with which Irwin is now arguing his case finally gets through to Charles. He had seen the state he was in in his cell and knows that, however bizarre it might seem, Irwin is telling the truth about the vest at least. And it all chimes with Jacqueline's account. He feels for him now, he hates what's happening in the room, feels complicit in something that's not fair, but nevertheless inevitable in its outcome. He says the only thing he can think of, 'And if it comes down to you or the local farmer Gaston, who do you think they are going to believe?'

'That's up to these gentlemen here.'

Ellwood is the judge, he doesn't seem to need a jury. He accuses Irwin of doing a great deal of harm to their relations with the town. He explains that they have already been in touch with the embassy. They are not sure how he sneaked into the country but they will ensure that he has the correct paperwork for his passage back to the United States. He will leave the moment the documents arrive. If he doesn't then he will be up before the court and he can rot in a French jail. In the meantime Mr. Dunham is kindly paying for a room in the hotel where he will remain until departure.

Fournier escorts him up to his new room. It's up three flights of stairs, each narrower than the one before, then along a dingy corridor that feels like the way to a whore's boudoir. He is surprised to see Sidonie waiting by one of the doors. Fournier instructs him to give all his clothes to her, speaks a few words to the girl in French then about turns and goes. She opens the door for him and they share an embarrassed moment of hesitation in the doorway. She won't go in but points to the bed, 'Une robe.' He steps into the tiny garret room. There's a gown on the bed, a little table with a crucifix and a candle. His valise is there, but also a tin bath full of water. 'Do I smell that bad?'

'Madame Dunham.'

That's all she says and pulls the door to. He undresses, feeling the slightest glimmer of hope that not everyone has abandoned him. He hands the clothes and the boots out to Sidonie, checking that she will bring them back, then asks after Jacqueline. She shakes her head.

'Convent?' he asks. She nods and tears stream down her face as she hurries away.

The warm water is the most soothing balm ever to wash over him. If only the tub was big enough he would happily drown in it. It would be the perfect, most peaceful end. He closes his eyes, so tired now...

When he opens them again, the water is cold… and red… He feels all over his body for the source of the blood. He stands up.

He's black and blue and raw where it looks like he's been dragged along the ground. There are deep red welts on both his shoulders and a brown stain covering his upper body. It won't rub off. His mood plunges as it dawns on him what it was that had so tainted his skin. *The vest... The vest, stolen, by him, stolen from him...* With that realisation comes a flood of guilt. He can see his pa, like he's angrily demanding to know where it is. He runs his hands despairingly through his hair. They find a massive lump on the back of his head and there's wet blood on his fingers. In the low-light of the room it looks almost black where it had been congealed around the wound. He plunges his head back into the tub. He does it once, he does it twice, the water growing ever more crimson. The third time he keeps his head submerged until it shoots out amid coughs, gasps and splutters. There is to be no easy way out. He dries himself off and stands naked by the tiny window that looks out over the town, the whole town; she's down there somewhere...

In the salon Irwin's heinous crime is the talk of the horse buyers enjoying an early evening aperitif. Charles doesn't particularly want to be there and is relieved when one of the staff tells him Mrs. Dunham would like to see him in the dining room. She's there with Virginia and the children. She wants to know if he's talked to Irwin, which he hasn't. She thinks Charles should know him better than anyone; does he believe he's done what they claim? Charles huffs and puffs, he knows that Carrie has had a soft spot for Irwin from day one. Part of him wants to smash any illusion she still has. After all she doesn't treat him, Charles, with the same respect, never looks at him in the same way, in fact she sometimes looks at him like he's boring and if he expresses an opinion she never seems impressed. At the same time she's a beautiful woman, absolutely adorable and he really wants her to like him. He confides in her what he really believes – that, however absurd it may seem, the story of the vest full of gold coins is true, he's certain of it.

'So did you say that – to Mr. Dunham and Mr. Ellwood?'

'No... I mean he still could have doped the horses.'

‘You believe so?’

‘Not *believe* no, I reckon he was with the girl.’

‘Did you say that? Did you defend him when you were in there?’

‘No.’

She sighs. ‘When you work at the bank Charles you will have people’s lives, their futures in your hands.’

‘You sound like my father.’

‘It’s too easy to go along with the mob.’

‘But… nobody asked me my opinion.’

She touches his arm and smiles, the human touch, the warmth of the gesture makes his day.

Irwin’s mind is awash with plans; he’s not done yet! So long as he’s got a plan he feels good. All that being sorry for himself, he’s over it and *once they bring my clothes back...* There’s a knock on the door, he leaps off his bed, expecting Sidonie. It’s Charles with a tray of food.

‘Where’s my clothes?’

‘Mrs. Dunham was concerned that you should have a proper meal.’

Seeing the food Irwin realises that he’s starving. He takes the tray and sits on the bed to eat. His gown hangs loose causing Charles to look away. He assures Irwin that the staff are laundering his clothes as fast as they can. That’s on the instructions of Mr. Ellwood himself who is adamant that Irwin should leave at the earliest opportunity.

‘And go where?’

‘Home Irwin, won’t it be good to go home and put this terrible business behind you?’

Irwin stops eating, surprised that Charles doesn’t understand. ‘I can never go home again. Don’t you see?’

‘Whyever not? If it’s a matter of finance I’m sure…’

‘What would I tell my pa? It was his gold. Going home without horses, it ain’t an option. I can’t go home!’

Charles has no answer to that, all he can say is that the paperwork is on its way. Irwin shakes his head and demands he has his clothes back, ‘You go tell ‘em to hurry along there, I got places to go!' Charles stops in the doorway, it's not his job to be jailer but... Irwin can't help smiling at the worried look now appearing on the man's face. 'You can come too Charlie...'

'Where are you going?'

'The fair. I like the fair, you wanna come?'

'The fair's gone.'

'Gone?'

That stops him smiling. The first of his plans was to find Gaston, hopefully in public – like in the bar at the fair, show him that he's not going away – he's onto him. And then he had other ideas... *Oh well...* He sucks on what feels like a rabbit bone.

'You know the song Charlie?' He sings quietly,

'Wake up, wake up darlin' Corrie
And go and get my gun
I ain't no hand for trouble
But I'll die before I run...
I'll die before I run.'

Irwin can't help a chuckle. Charles is looking even more worried.

'I ain't running nowhere Charlie, it ain't the American way – you should know that – no duty to retreat an' all that? But don't look so scared – I ain't got a gun. Not yet...'

Taking his clothes was a clever move. With his boots on he'd be down that farm, have Gaston by the throat, the odds are the critter would still have the gold; he wouldn't dare show it – not for a while. There was still hope. If only he could get dressed! He's tempted to shout down the landing, shout out of the window, but what's the point when the whole world's against you? He paces the room as the light fades, wishing he could be like the Sioux, calm and still. He tries it, it doesn't work. The next knock on the door still doesn't deliver his clothes. It's Sidonie to bring him water and hand over a note. He lights the candle. There's a moment of hope; a note always offers the possibility of good news, but it's not to be. It simply begins, '*Just so you know...*' and tells him that he will be leaving on a train for

Le Havre in the morning. There he will be met by an agent who will hand over travel documents, including a Passe Provisoire that will enable him to make the journey home. That's all, It's not signed, but he's intrigued - it's on hotel paper with the dolphin crest embossed on the top and it's written in a fine hand. When he holds the paper to his nose, he recognises the perfume. Why has she done that? Has Charles told her he has no intention of going home? Is she warning him? He looks out onto the landing but Sidonie has gone, there's not a soul around.

'My clothes!!'

He shouts into the darkness, but to no avail.

He's standing at the window as the very first light of day picks out the silhouettes of the town roofs. It will soon be dawn and then what? He hears a creaking on the landing and creeps across to the door. Whoever it is he'll grab them, do whatever; have the clothes off their back if he has to… He pulls open the door as Sidonie is setting his clothes down on the floor. She lets out a little yelp, startled, expecting him to be sleeping. 'Shhh…' He calms her and thanks her, gathers up the bundle and shuts the door.

He lights the candle. His clothes have never felt so good. His boots have a shine. The suit is still warm and smells of woodsmoke from where they've dried it by the fire. He dresses as fast as he can, but his feet don't fit the boots. He curses, tipping them up; bread and cheese drop on to the floor. He has to bite his lip and stifle the tear that wells up out of nowhere – *The generous will themselves be blessed for they share their food with the poor… Sidonie…* tears are running down his face, he can't help it. *You're not on your own…* He'd not felt able to face his mother, shame had pushed family from his mind but now he can feel her with him. *Thank you.* He puts the food in his jacket pocket and picks out the only thing left in his valise – his old battered hat. It had served him well, but seen better days and he'd not worn it since his arrival at the hotel for fear that it would give him away – mistake! He sticks it firmly on his head, feeling it passing over the lump. It's his lucky hat, it was who he was, now he can be himself. He creeps out of the room and down the stairs. He can hear one or two early morning voices in the kitchen as he crosses the yard. There's something energising about the cool fresh air, the feel of a new day. The stable boys are still asleep but wake when he starts to put a saddle on Blanche. He says 'Hi' and takes out the note Sidonie had handed to him the night before and waves it in front of them. They can't read it of course, but he makes sure they see the hotel crest and he uses a lot of words like 'important' and 'Ellwood' knowing they haven't a clue what he's talking about. It's a good performance, so good that they help him with the bridle and adjusting the stirrups. While they're doing that he slips a handy hoof knife into his pocket. They ask a lot of questions which he deliberately fails to understand and after much shrugging he waves them goodbye and is soon heading at a steady canter out of town.

By the time he comes near Gaston's commune the whole world seems to be awake, even the church bell is tolling and farm workers have looked up from their work as he's passed, which isn't helpful. He heads for the same overgrown track where he suspects he's going to have to lie low. Blanche is not keen, memories of being abandoned here are not forgotten. He understands - his own flashbacks are stabbing at his guts. He coaxes her gently between hanging branches, until brambles bar their way and they can go no further. She's soon happily distracted by the feast of leaves that surround her. He realises it could be a long day but at least he won't be on that train. He finds a gap in the hedge where he can see across the field. Is she somewhere over there or already in the convent? He can glimpse various people coming and going, but the buildings obscure his view. He can hear men shouting which makes him wonder how many work at the farm. His hand feels for the hoof-knife for reassurance. *'Hell's teeth!'* Suddenly men are coming beyond the buildings looking in his direction. Two of them have shotguns. He ducks down, this could spell disaster – the one thing he must avoid is being caught. Word must have got to Gaston – of course it had! Field labourers had seen him coming. He starts to lead the horse away. A shot rings out, alarming her. Irwin throws himself into the saddle and she takes no bidding to run for her life as more shots ring out. When they reach the road, someone is heading their way at a gallop. Irwin curses, but he's in luck - Blanche takes off like she's leader of the pack; no skinny half-breed is going to come anywhere near. When they reach a sharp bend, the horse that wouldn't cross a tramline takes him clean over a hedge, hurtling straight on across fields, through a stream and up into a wood. Only then can Irwin get her to slow down. Any pursuer they may have had is left way out of sight. He dismounts, hugs and kisses her, touches his hat to her, sure that she had understood and had done what they needed to do. They get their breath back. A warm feeling creeps over him, he can't help it – this is the life he knows and loves, just him and a horse, better than a goddamn human any day!

NINE

It seems to be a wood rather than a forest, they pass through and into another valley and find a stream where they both drink. Irwin sits chewing on the bread and cheese. He finally works out what's so different today – it's the lightness. The vest had become a part of him and without it his body feels strange. *The gold.* It's what brought him here and it's why he can't leave. It's a curse. He could be on the boat now, going home… The horse nuzzles him. 'So little lady, you're going to have to tell… what the hell we going to do now?'

It always intrigued Irwin the way stuff happened, be it his mother watching over him or just something bigger than all of them, playing them like fools. It was like you were nothing out there – a tiny speck and yet somehow you were always in some bigger picture; neither you nor nothing else was random, he knew it but he couldn't get a hang of it. That's how it is now when he lets Blanche take him who knows where? They come to a place he's been before. How was that? Did she know it too? It was back on a main road, there were carts and coaches and she trotted on like she knew exactly where she was heading. Then he recognised the road-side inn; 'Auberge' was painted on the wall; 'Auberge de la Grâce de Dieu.' It was where they'd stopped en-route to that Bonheur woman's place, where they rested up the horses. Blanche heads straight for the water trough. Irwin can see heads turning; a group of men animatedly complaining about their lot, as working men do, now stop to look – does he really look so foreign? Is it natural curiosity or have they read the newspapers – is he a headline already, a wanted man? It's enough to make him nervous. He lets Blanche drink then kicks her on. He pats her mane and sings her praises, thanks her a hundred times – he now knows exactly where they're going.

The road to Rosa Bonheur's, he remembers by the milestones, is also the road to Paris. That doesn't interest him but he has a growing feeling that this was all meant to be. He can hear his mother's voice – *'You know where you should be – you should be in the circus!'* and that's just what he's going to do – join Bill Cody's Wild West Show! There's a moment of questioning as they trot along, *And where's that going to get you?* But it's outweighed by a wave of excitement. It's crazy and it's wonderful all at the same time.

The villagers in one of the communes that the road passes through are stopped in their tracks when a riderless horse gallops towards them. Suddenly Irwin appears from the side, swings into the saddle, then stands on poor Blanche's rump for a few moments before dropping back down, waving his hat to the locals and heading on through. He apologises to the horse – he's a bit rusty and he's never done it with a saddle on before. 'We got a lot to work at, you and me!' When he was a kid his folks had taken him to another Wild West Show and after that they couldn't stop him trick riding round the paddock. He's now heading for a dream come true! Cody will pay him and he'll go back and somehow get Jacqueline. There's plenty of time to think while they're eating up the miles and the girl starts to feel more important even than the horses. They had something special he knows it – he'd never felt nothing like that, not for any girl he'd ever known. He can still feel it now, a feeling so strong that he starts to feel like she's a magnet and he's riding in the wrong direction, but he's got to do it! Without money he's nothing.

Paris is much further than he expected. They ride all day until Blanche makes it quite clear she's had enough. When he stops and asks someone how far it is to Paris they look at him like they've never heard of it. There's only so many ways you can pronounce P A R I S - it's not a hopeful sign. Then comes the rain driving across a flat boring plain. When the road descends to a river he decides that has to be it for the day. There are mills and farms in the valley and some have stuff growing in their gardens. He comes to a village that seems dead to the world even before the light has faded. He finds a little pond on the outskirts, with trees and plenty of fresh grass. He tethers Blanche where she can eat and drink and heads off to find his supper. Some cottages have neat little potagers – well tended vegetable gardens, but what is there that he can eat? He spots rhubarb - pie-plant he calls it. As soon as it's dark and all lights are out, he creeps into the garden, folds up one of the large leaves into a pouch, takes a bite of the rhubarb, winces at its bitterness and then moves round collecting anything that looks edible and putting it in the pouch. It's a poor harvest, nothing seems quite ready for picking, the most edible leaf tastes of cabbage. Everything he picks from the fruit trees is hard and sour. He wanders silently through the village. There's a boulangerie which he thinks offers the best hope. He finds his way round the back and sure enough there's a basket of stale bread. He goes back to Blanche who likes the rock-hard bread more than he does, but he eats it anyway. Like every village he's passed this one has the lavoir – the covered shelter on the edge of the pond where he'd seen women gather to do their washing. At least it's out of the rain. He tethers Blanche to the corner post and tries to sleep.

It's a lousy night. His clothes are damp, his stomach cramps and complains, he succumbs to exhaustion and is out of it for a while but then a million thoughts and fears race through his semi-conscious mind. The worst nightmare is when he sees his mother and she's mad at him, mad at him for destroying his poor, righteous father. How dare she? *It wouldn't have happened if you hadn't gone and died – none of this! Why did you leave me!!* And he wakes so angry with his mother. It takes him a moment to even work out where he is. He'd never fallen out with his mother, what was happening? Even now he was awake she feels so real, like she's there with him. It haunts him as he untethers Blanche and sets off once again. It's the truth – if his mother was still alive he'd still be in Kansas. She'd have been there and that would have been enough. Blanche insists on grabbing some leaves from the hedgerow as they leave the village. He lets her, the row with his mother sapping his energy as it fills him with remorse. Such an odd day with the dream more real than the alien landscape around him. *Where the hell am I?* He idly picks and eats a couple of leaves himself and then a few berries that look like raisins, there are red ones and black ones, he's tasted worse. He puts some in his pouch before forcing Blanche to trot on. She's reluctant to rejoin the main road but once he's coaxed her there's no stopping her. She has a compulsion to never let another horse overtake her. Irwin loves her spirit but fears she won't last the day and sometimes is forced to turn off in order to let a coach thunder by.

His spirits soar when another coach passes flying two flags – one is American the other he recognises from the fair in Nogent – it's the bright yellow and reds of the Wild West Show. He lets out a mighty whoop that startles Blanche and sends her off in hot pursuit. She's one wild horse that's finally found someone as crazy as she is. He rides, head low, talking to her as they go, holding her back a little, explaining that this could still be a long ride and you don't always have to be out in front to win the race.

TEN

Jacqueline sits quietly in the back of the mule cart, letting herself be taken up the hill towards the oldest part of the town. It's not completely new to her but it remains unfamiliar with a rarefied atmosphere that's different to the rest of Nogent. The only people she sees go silently about their business and the horse's hooves echo off the walls. There's no render on the buildings up here, only the bleak stonework of the church of Saint-Laurent, and then next to it the college. She looks up to a little window above the archway that spans the road – is some lucky young man studying in there? Emerging on the other side they're passing the court house and the prison. She smiles - they may as well stop there, but they don't. Gaston, her aunt and her uncle, all squashed on the driving seat, carry on to the next bleak edifice with its own heavy iron bars on the windows. It was known to every girl in the Perche – *'You behave or you'll end up in Le Bon Pasteur.'* Jacqueline sighs as the cart comes to a halt. She tells herself to stay calm although her heart is beating hard in her chest. She's stopped fighting, she knows she's no physical match for the animal strength of her cousin. Even his mother and father are frightened of him, but she'll die before she marries him. Maybe that will be her final choice, but not yet, for now she'll bide her time. It's all to play for so long as you're smart.

Beyond the heavy oak door, with its tiny metal grill, the four of them are led by one of the nuns past a candle-lit statue of the Virgin Mary and paintings of various saints, to the office of the Reverend Mother. The first surprise is that the woman isn't even French, she appears to be some sort of Prussian. Jacqueline can see that this does not sit well with the family – it's not that long ago that they were at war with them. They are even less happy to hear that they will be expected to pay towards Jacqueline's keep. Gaston protests – he had been told that all the girls worked making shirts. The protest gets him nowhere but makes Jacqueline smile – he's no longer talking about her staying until she's twenty-one but hopes that a short time in the convent will help her learn penitence, turn away from the temptations of the flesh and embrace the Lord. This from a man who had told his parents God didn't exist and had thrown a crucifix at his father in a drunken rage. Now he's crossing himself and trying to make out the devil has possessed his intended bride and he fears for her soul. Jacqueline can tell that the Reverend Mother can see through him, the arrogance of her manner was definitely Prussian and she looked like she despised all peasants. When she makes the assumption that Jacqueline is illiterate and unable to sign the pledge of obedience for herself, Jacqueline has had enough; she refuses to be treated as a commodity that no one even looks at. She breaks her silence and insists that she can both read and write. The enormous wimple now turns in her direction for the first time. The room becomes silent as the two women stare into each other's eyes. The Reverend Mother wants to know if this is trouble arriving; the intelligent ones corrupt the other girls and cause discontent. Jacqueline, without saying another word, wants to make it clear that she's not, as Gaston implied, some slut who will lift her skirt for any man. Eventually the Reverend Mother turns her gaze back to the papers on her desk and starts again at the beginning of the script that she recites to all new-comers. To enter the penitent will have to sign a declaration that she wishes to leave vice behind and embrace penitence and absolute obedience. All penitents are forbidden to speak of their life outside in the world, the penitence of a daughter of the Good Shepherd consists of assiduous work. She will therefore be expected to work hard, the food will be minimal and coarse and strict silence will be observed at all times except during periods of recreation. When she's finished the woman looks at Jacqueline daring her to make a challenge. She pushes the paper towards her and Jacqueline signs without a word of protest. She notices that her uncle's lip is trembling. He's a good man but weak and she knows he has found the whole business unbearable. Now he and his wife are the ones, as her guardians, who have to sign. A tear drips from his nose onto the paper much to the Reverend Mother's disgust. She then tells the trio that they may leave. None of them can look at Jacqueline. She pulls her uncle back and hugs him, forcing a smile to assure him it's going to be okay. That's the only moment her eyes water – his pain weakens her. She turns away and stares at the ceiling.

A young woman wearing a black woollen dress escorts Jacqueline silently to what feels like a store room. Once inside she introduces herself in a hushed voice as Rose, but in the convent she is known as Acquilina and Jacqueline will be given her own saint's name later. For now she has to undress and put on the costume of a penitent. As she does so Rose quietly tells her the nuns to avoid and the girls who'll betray you to them. She's a little confused – if Jacqueline isn't an unmarried mother and if she's not a prostitute then why is she there? Rose can sense the venom as Jacqueline explains her situation and she warms to her. She assures her she will be fine; the only girls there who lack all respect are the ones who repent their sins. They're no fun at all! And at least she has a way out, some of the poor women are there for life and you get no letters, no presents and you're not even allowed to send letters out. So, Jacqueline wonders, what about Rose - is she there for life? Rose smiles, she's made 'friends' with the priest, he's promised he will get her a position in the seminary kitchen. She raises her arms in a *why not* gesture – one cock's the same as any other! Jacqueline laughs for the first time in days.

It was a different sort of cold in the convent. Stone cold from the lime-washed walls and flagstone floors and ice cold from the lack of human warmth. That was the chill that went right through her as she took her place in the hall for her first meal, the cold, colourless, silent girls – some so young, heads shorn, all wearing the same woollen dresses. Starved of who they were, reduced to who the sisters wanted them to be. This reality disturbed her more than any fears she had had of what lay in store. There seemed to be a hierarchy; there were the nuns, then there were those girls whose families had given them up to be nuns; the novices, they wore different head-dresses, then there were the rest – by far the greatest number, the girls 'saved' from the streets, from destitute parents, or those who had brought shame on their families - these had trouped last into the hall. The food was bread and a watery broth. That didn't bother her, it was what she'd expected, but to remain silent in such repressed company was against her nature and she could feel her anger brewing. At the end of the meal she is summoned to the front to be formally introduced. The Reverend Mother proceeds to tell the story of Saint Isadora the Simple who was ridiculed by the other nuns for wearing a dishrag on her head instead of a veil, but when a Holy hermit visited he saw not a dishrag but a bright glow around her head – she had been marked out by the Lord, whereupon the other nuns fell to their knees and begged forgiveness. Isadora, with true humility rejected such adulation and spent the rest of her life as a hermit. Advising Jacqueline that we all need to learn humility, she introduces her to the hall as Isadora. One of the nuns then comes forward to cut her hair. Luckily Rose had warned her that it was one of many customs of the convent that were frowned upon by the government. Jacqueline raises her voice and her hands to object. The nun looks to the Reverend Mother, who quietly reminds the newcomer of the pledge she had signed and almost shouts to the hall to heed the sin of pride. The nun approaches once again with the scissors. Jacqueline grabs her wrist and turns to the Reverend Mother, 'Personne ne me coupe les cheveux!' No one cuts my hair! The Reverend Mother has years of experience of rebellion and knows when and when not to react. She smiles at Jacqueline and tells her she may return to her seat. Both Jacqueline and the Reverend Mother know this is but the start of a duel, one which both will relish. The Reverend Mother kicks it off with a sour tasting homily warning them all that there's a very good reason why the Bible never says what the devil looks like; it is because he comes to them in many guises. She quotes Corinthians, 'Satan himself masquerades as an angel of light.' She doesn't stop until she feels that she has said enough to convince the vulnerable that Jacqueline is but the devil's latest manifestation and should be avoided at all cost. The sadness for Jacqueline is that many seem to believe her and her act of rebellion has not won her any friends. Those close to her in the dormitory won't even look at her. Were they really so afraid? Do they believe all the fearmongering lies? Or did they simply not want trouble? Only Rose on the far side of the room looks across to her, puts her hands together in front of her face and behind the hands, smiles broadly. That's enough, Jacqueline responds with the same gesture. She needed to know she wasn't alone.

*****

Back in Kansas the note Irwin wrote before boarding the train was finally picked up by his father when he'd gone into town. It was short and full of false optimism. Irwin had sworn on his mother's life that he would come back with horses. '*Trust me!!*' Now weeks had gone by and the atmosphere on the farm was increasingly desolate. Hopes that he'd see sense and return had faded. Mary-Ann is frequently overcome with tears of rage, not believing that her brother could stoop so low. Abe has withdrawn more and more into himself. Lying awake at night he convinces himself that he now knows the culprit – it was the gold. *Gold!* What was it about gold that drove men crazy? He's sure Irwin wouldn't have taken his money if it was cash. He'd handled large sums over the years, trading the horses and had always played it straight. What was he now going to do with a vest full of Double Eagles? *It was the gold – he couldn't resist the gold.* He'd known so many men driven crazy by it, he thought he'd turned it his way, overcome its curse, but then he'd unburied the demon, leaving the family on the brink of ruin. *Gold...*

When he's out working Abe carries the note with him. He's read it many times and all day long his eyes keep drifting to the horizon. Sometimes he stops work all together and stands staring, watching, waiting – what else can he do?

*****

Irwin keeps up the encouraging words as Blanche eats up the miles. He needs to convince himself as much as her. The ride seems to be going on forever. It moves him how this out of condition misfit, confined to the stables because she couldn't be trusted, now just keeps on going. Irwin feels like she knows what is needed from her, can feel his desperation. She's a strong-willed horse, could refuse to go another step if she so decided. Maybe she also has somewhere she's heading. Whatever it is, the two of them, totally exhausted, now travel as one.

The flag carrying coach and four has long since left them behind, but people they pass tell them they're heading in the right direction. The Wild West poster back in Nogent had said 'Paris' and the ever increasing traffic heading that way keeps them going. Irwin hears their destination before he sees any sign of it. The road is emerging from a forest when a familiar sound is carried on the wind – it's a band playing the 'Star Spangled Banner.' At first he doesn't believe it, it only comes in faint waves, like a cruel trick of the mind, but then there are echoing gunshots. He lets out a 'whoop' that spurs Blanche once again into a canter. 'Injuns – over the bluff! Let's get'em girl!' There is no losing the way now, coaches of every description are heading in only one direction. They are forced to slow down as they approach an archway constructed over the entrance to a park, 'Buffalodorum' it says in huge letters. It's the greatest number of people Irwin has seen since he left New York – far more than at the fair in Nogent and the park is the biggest he's ever seen. Hundreds of people are disembarking from coaches and ahead of them he can see army tents, tepees, enclosures with buffalo and elk, many American flags and the music is now loud and clear. Irwin dismounts and leads Blanche through the crowds. He can hear American voices urging people to hurry to see the show. Others are selling Stetson hats. Everything is now American, there are even long-bearded frontiersmen wandering around. It's like he's come home and yet… he doesn't feel the elation he imagined he would feel when the idea first took hold. For a start now he's walking his legs feel shaky after so long in the saddle and his stomach isn't so good either – in fact he feels sick as a dog. He dips his hand into the pouch remembering he hasn't eaten in hours. Blanche has the last bit of bread leaving only leaves and berries. The horse leads him to a camp of Mexican vacqueros - cowboys all saddling up. It's the drinking trough she's after. Irwin watches, the scale of the whole operation is blowing his mind and causing the knot in his stomach to tighten. Once the Mexicans start moving off as a troupe he drags Blanche away from the water and they follow. They join up with about fifty cavalry mounted soldiers. From another direction come the same number of Sioux warriors in full battledress. Then Irwin hears the brass band approaching. They too are on horseback. They've all come together and the horses whinny and call to each other, restless, raring to go. Blanche is becoming tense and Irwin holds her on a short rein making comforting noises, assuring her he's there. The band stops playing. There's that eerie calm that follows; a silent anticipation, before Irwin sees the man himself approaching – Buffalo Bill comes riding on his white horse to take his place at the head of the procession. There's a sense of awe runs through the crowd. This is not the *common as an old shoe* Bill Cody that Irwin had recounted to Rosa Bonheur, this is man elevated to myth. He raises his arm and with a single gesture the band strikes up and the parade sets off towards the show ring. Behind those on horseback there are families of settlers on foot and Sioux women and children. Most of those watching follow, but Irwin somehow can't. He sits on a bank, unable to even stay on his feet. He's annoyed with himself. He should be over the moon. What is it that's twisting his gut? In the distance he hears the Star Spangled Banner once again, *Come on this is good – you're home!* But he's not home at all. That's the point, he's never been further from home, he'd deceived himself once again and now he's here it's a new reality. This is not the start of another glorious adventure, this is a desperate attempt to save his skin, stop himself from starving even, and he's not sure how he's going to do it. It's his mother's anger that still hangs over him, dulling his spirits; a judgement from the one person that never judged. *What was he thinking? What had he been thinking all along?* Those were her words in the dream and they haunt him now.

He sits for hours feeling increasingly ill and more and more detached from the people passing by. He's aware of distant battles taking place in the show ring, fusillades of shots being fired and the whoops and cries of the Indian warriors. The commentator's voice rises and falls on the wind. A Yankee voice far away… home… far away… Blanche crops the grass all around them. She's right there but everything starts to feel far, far away.

A band is playing, it's getting louder, coming closer. Blanche becomes restless, nervous, forcing Irwin to his feet. The show; it must be over, the cavalry go past, then the vacqueros and the Indians. Finally Irwin sees Bill Cody flanked by outriders. 'Come on now…' He forces himself to follow. More and more of the parade peel off to their various camps until only Cody's little party remain. Irwin keeps following. They go down an avenue of ever grander tents with fences and shrubs outside. Some are draped with buffalo skins and have carpets leading inside. At the end of the avenue is the biggest tent of all with a buffalo head above the entrance. Cody dismounts and talks to a man in a top hat. Irwin makes his move, 'Excuse me sir, Colonel Cody sir…'

The man in the top hat intervenes, 'Not now lad!'

Irwin ignores him, 'I was wondering if you had anything going in the line of work. I can trick ride, I've been round horses all my life, First word ever came out of my mouth was 'horse'.'

'Sorry son' And Cody was looking at him now.

'But I seen action! I was a scout for the 6th cavalry. I'm a pretty mean shot.'

'Is that so? Problem is we got us a full troupe.' He hands his horse to a groom and heads for his tent. Irwin is slurring now, 'I'm begging you sir! I need work and I need it bad!'

Cody has stopped and looks at Irwin again, studies him for a moment, 'Do I know you?'

'My cousin was with you sir – at War Bonnet Creek. Spoke highly of you sir…'

'Mr Salsbury…' Cody looks to his manager and disappears inside.

'There's no work son, and that is it.' With that Salsbury follows Cody into the tent.

The world is starting to come and go, Irwin grabs onto Blanche, hauls himself onto the saddle, aware that people are watching. Everything is spinning around. Irwin lies forward kicking into her flanks, trying to get away from somewhere, from tents that keep coming and going, people shouting. Blanche is panicking unsure what is going on, turns away from the sound of rifle shots, starts to get skittish, wanting away from the crowds. Irwin's head is lying on her mane. He can see tepees and squaws and Indian children and panics as the world goes sideways, *Where the heck..?* A searing pain grips his gut and he feels himself falling from his horse.

ELEVEN

Irwin is aware of his own voice screaming somewhere far away. He's begging forgiveness as the Indian holds him to the ground closing in now to scalp him… but no - the man's huge fingers are forcing themselves down his throat, the eternal fires are burning inside him and below him, it's the blackness of the Normandie dungeon lit only by the flames that are now raging, spewing from his own mouth as he passes through the red-hot grating, heading for the furnace, down and down... His head explodes, 'Jacqueline! Jed! Ma, where are you?' He can see them all in the fire and there's his little brother and sister but they do nothing to help him. Poison is being poured into him by the huge hands, he chokes and splutters; *they're drowning me!* Then the flames come again, his insides pouring out of him. There are more of them now holding him, turning him so he can't see their evil faces but he's above them now, his mother's there, then she's gone, he's calling to her, he's calling to her, begging her to come back…

The torment is never ending, he passes over but it's no escape. He's back seeing Indian warriors stripping the clothes from his back, then their women are mouthing curses, others are singing the death song. He forces open his eyes and they're still there, threatening him in the shadow-filled darkness. *Where am I?*

It's an age before the pains subside and he comes back from somewhere, opening his eyes again to the flickering of a lamp. Water is being offered, a damp cloth laid on his forehead. In time he trusts them, reassured by the unmistakeable smell of the inside of a tent. But the song? A wave of panic grips him, he can hear the low murmur of the singing that he'd heard before. He tries to sit up and speak, 'Death song?'

It's a woman who's sitting beside him singing softly. She doesn't understand him and leaves the tent. The Indian that comes back with her he recognises although he can't place him. The man leans over him, 'Welcome back.'

'Death song?'

'No…'

Irwin can see him more clearly now, his eyes adjusting to the lamp light. The man is saying something in his own language.

'Not the Death song?'

The man shakes his head.

He closes his eyes and lets himself drift away.

He comes to in daylight to the sound of children's laughter. One of them sees him staring at them and runs out of the tent. The others sit watching him. When he says 'hello' his voice is unfamiliar - weak and hoarse. He still feels strange, totally confused… To his horror he finds he's naked under the blanket. The child returns with a man. This time he recognises him – it's the Sioux warrior from the fair, 'Nogent!'

The man nods.

'What the hell's going on?'

The man comes down to Irwin's level and picks up the rhubarb leaf pouch which is lying by the blanket. He opens it up and there are some squashed berries inside, 'You eat?'

'Sure I did! I had to get what I could.'

The man shakes his head.

'Poison?'

And he nods. Irwin is relieved.

'Bad medicine.'

'You're not fucking kidding me!'

The full horror of the night soon becomes apparent. As well as the hallucinations Irwin had lost control of all bodily functions. These people had kindly cleaned him up. His clothes are outside now, drying in the sun. Others of the tribe soon come to look, particularly the women. They'd given him their medicine to purge him and they make out he's lucky to be alive. They're Oglala Sioux from South Dakota. Irwin wonders what they're doing here – particularly as the man, whose name translates as

Red Shirt seemed to be so bitter against the white man when he'd seen him at the fair. He regrets asking. It's like Red Shirt has been waiting all his life to tell his story. He was sent to Nogent because he spoke some French - he'd been with the tribe when they'd fled to Canada during the Black Hills war. He also spoke better English than most in the camp. He uses it to lecture his still nauseous captive audience on the sad fate of his people; how their land had been stolen, how the white man had broken every treaty they made and were not to be trusted. He tells of how they'd been forced onto reservations where they were not allowed to speak their own language or even wear tribal dress; of how they were forced to live on food hand-outs from the white man and accept the white-man's god. After what feels like an hour or two of a tragic history he finally gets to the point – they're with the show because here they are free to be themselves, speak their own language, follow their own customs, their tribal dances, wear their own clothes. They are paid and Cody sends money back to their families. In addition to that the French people are kind, they call them, 'Les Américains qui disparaîtront,' *The Americans who will vanish* – because they know that is what the Americans are trying to do – 'That is why they hunted the buffalo to extinction – so we would have no food.' Irwin thinks back to two young Lakota lads who had run away from the reservation. He knows Red Shirt's stories are true. The two boys had told him the same. They had left to live the life they had always known, that was now denied them. They joined up with him rounding up mustangs. They were brilliant on horseback and had taught him so much. They had had a great two weeks until they came across an army patrol on the lookout for Indians who had attacked some gold miners. They tied the boys up and Irwin watched them having to run behind the horses as they were taken back to the reservation. He felt sick that he did nothing to help them. Instead he proudly took home a string of mustangs and had never spoken of the incident since. Shame. Now their people had saved his life.

His nakedness has a disturbing precedent. He keeps asking after his clothes until one of the men brings him a pair of his own buckskin trousers and a top. It causes much amusement once he puts it on, but he doesn't care - it allows him to venture gingerly out of the tent. It's blindingly bright! Blanche is tethered nearby and seems content, if a little unsure when she sees him. He assures her they're going nowhere. The kids that have been charged with looking after her are grooming her straggly mane and she seems like she has new friends. He leaves them to it, moving through the camp. He keeps having to stop to take it all in. It's different somehow – is that tepee really there? Of course it is, but at the same time… Has something happened to his brain? Is it the sun or are the colours sharper? There are waves of something like panic, of not trusting what he's seeing. He has to go back and lie down, frightened. The camp empties as everyone goes off to do a show. Irwin huddles under his blanket, still not sure what's real and what isn't, something has blurred the lines. It gets even weirder when French people start looking into the tent. After the show there are even more of them wandering round the camp. He goes outside and whole families are there, pointing things out to their children – pointing *him* out! They say 'Bonjour' and smile, have their photograph taken next to him. He can only nod, not daring to speak; he's an exotic exhibit and he doesn't want to disillusion them. After the second show Red Shirt comes to him, bringing him food. Until now he had not even asked Irwin to tell his story which now strikes him as odd. 'Don't you want to know why I'm here?'

Red Shirt looks at him, he thinks he knows his story   he had watched him in Nogent – he was always alone. Then he arrived here in the camp and he saw him again - *alone*. He puts his hand to his heart… 'No one was singing the Death Song; what you heard was the Song of Pity; a prayer to Wakan Tanka asking that you be guided home to your people.' Irwin feels the wetness of a tear on his cheek. He buries his head in the blanket. He has little control over his emotions. He struggles to pull himself together. He starts to tell Red Shirt why he can't go home, avoiding any mention of the gold. He had heard prospectors in bars back home bragging about gun battles with Indians who had claimed they were trespassing on their land. One even had a gruesome souvenir taken from a boy he'd killed. So he only tells half a tale but Red Shirt looks at him like he knows, like he's waiting for the real reason he didn't take the boat back home. Bit by bit Irwin tells how it was his father's life savings that he'd taken, how he thought he could save the family. Finally, unnerved by the gaze that goes right through him, he admits that the savings were all in gold coins.

Red Shirt says nothing. When this man talks it goes on forever, but when he's silent it also speaks volumes. He looks straight ahead as he'd done when Irwin first met him and Irwin is at one with the man's thoughts. He closes his eyes and can see it all; he can feel the gold now like it's being melted. Is that Gaston melting it down even now? The molten metal is pouring back through time, through the vest, through his burnt hands, through his father's hands, back into the land, the land they didn't own. When he opens his eyes Red Shirt is still there.

'So you have betrayed the trust of your father?'

Irwin is no longer sure who he's betrayed but he nods. 'How can I go home?'

*****

The big German has Irwin by the throat. He has no idea what he's done until he sees the other men falling about laughing. The frontiersmen are a rough and ready bunch, recruited from those laid off at the end of a cattle drive. For the first time since arriving in France, Irwin had felt a different kind of ease – these were his own countrymen, speaking his kind of language. They were not big-time dealers, he's now with the sort of men he's used to from the frontier towns. It's thanks to Rocky Bear, the leader of Oglalas in the camp; he had put a word in for him and the next morning Irwin had found himself mucking out horses in the main stables. Then one of the men had told him to go and call Arschloch the German. He had no idea it wasn't his name – that he was calling him 'ass'ole.' It's all a great laugh and Irwin can take a joke, it's like his initiation. It's all good - he has his own clothes back and he's feeling a million times better in his head. Added to that he's with guys who are having the time of their lives – telling Irwin of the wonders of Paris – not the famous new tower but the whores! When the mucking out's done they take him to their camp. Irwin can't believe the scale of the show. He knew there were over 150 horses but now he's walking past a herd of buffalo, then there's elk and Texas longhorn cattle. He stops to take it all in. He's told it's the biggest show in the world and he can believe it. They move on to roped off areas where men are practising – there's bucking broncos, rope tricks and bareback riders. One of the men, Evert, asks Irwin if he can shoot. Irwin thinks *money!* He needs to make money - the old Irwin is suddenly back offering to take any of them on if they're up for a wager. Evert claims they'd love to but don't have live ammunition. However there's a sharpshooter in the show, who shoots clays, they'll take him on. Before he can say anything Evert calls to a couple standing talking by a clay trap, 'Heh Phoebe!' The woman turns, 'This gentleman's newly arrived – Mr Irwin Gurd, from Kansas, he fancies taking you on!' Irwin protests, he's never shot against a woman! But one of the others shuts him up, tells him she needs putting in her place, 'She thinks she's bloody Annie Oakley!' They go under the rope and walk across to the couple as the men assure him that shooting clays is easy. They ask her if he can have a practise shot. The gentleman with her is introduced as Phoebe's husband Frank Butler. He has two long wires which, when Irwin is ready, he pulls to trigger the trap. Irwin misses first time, then gets his eye in on the second shot. He's soon confident and they all start talking about the form of the competition, how much he wants to wager – he'll be paid at the end of the week, so he can do that, and how much they are going to bet themselves. The woman looks uneasy and asks if she can have a practise too. There's a chorus of 'No!' from the men. The woman loads her gun, looks at the men, springs the trap herself, spins round and still hits the clay. Irwin stands, open mouthed.

'Annie Oakley… Nice to meet you Mr. Gurd.'

'You're Annie Oakley?'

'You be careful -these men are not to be trusted!' While the men moan about her spoiling their fun, Annie – real name Phoebe Ann Mosy – continues with her practise session. Irwin watches her husband walk away, then he holds a target at arm's length.

She stands with her back to him, aims the gun over her shoulder, takes aim, using only a small mirror to see the target and fires – and hits the target, not the husband! Irwin is left, once again, open-mouthed. The men rib him and suggest he could try that – it's with a proper rifle, if he's as good as he says he is… They carry on to their camp. Irwin won't be bragging anymore to these guys.

He watches the show in the afternoon. It's in a big arena with a huge canvas backdrop of the Rocky Mountains. His mother was right – this is like everything Irwin ever wanted to do in his life – and you're paid for it – paid for showing off! There's plenty of trick riding, sharp shooting, guns being fired all over the place, there's Indians chasing buffalo, there's an attack on a settler's cabin, an attack on a stage coach – the occupants of both saved by the heroic cavalry riding to the rescue and it all culminates in Custer's Last Stand – with Bill Cody playing General Custer of course. Irwin's adrenalin is pumping – *I could do that!* - one way or another he's going to be in this show. He thanks his mother – she's the one who has guided him here, he knows it – this is meant to be!

After the show he has to help with the stabling of the horses. In this little microcosm he's conscious of how many different accents and tongues he's hearing as the men unsaddle their rides. There's north European, Irish, Scottish, the Spanish of the vacqueros and of course the Lakota of the Oglalas. Irwin talks to as many of them as he can, ultimately looking for a way in, but the various groups stick to themselves as they go off to their different camps. It's a bit of a let down, it's only the wild but welcoming frontiersmen that urge him to join them – they've got plenty of drink, although the way they tell it, it's like it is not encouraged by the show. It's a one-performance day so the whole evening lies ahead of him, but when his work is done he surprises himself by turning them down. Yes he was tempted by the invitation to play cards but after the Annie Oakley ruse he doesn't trust them. One or two of them, for all the laughter, he could now tell, were bitter – he could see it in their eyes and he knew they somehow resented his youth. If he won and he knew he was good, it would mean trouble. That was one lesson he'd learned back home. Were these excuses? What he's not admitting to himself is that his confidence is not what it should be. Something did happen in his brain that night and it's left his grip on things not so good. It comes in waves, verging on panic, with him feeling like he's close to the edge and if he crosses a line, he will be gone forever. It's only a moment but he has to stop, fix his eyes on something, convince himself it's real. It had happened when Evert talked to him about going to the brothels in Paris. A knot in his stomach; was it the word 'Paris' or 'brothel'? The idea of going out of the camp? Time was he'd have jumped at the chance, he'd always liked to try what a new town had to offer, but he had to walk away, stand watching a flag blowing in the wind. It passed after a minute and it was Jacqueline that came to him in the void. Evert was behind him, 'You been to a whore house before ain't you?'

Jacqueline was there, thumping him in the guts; '*Remember me?'*

Where was she? Right now, as he thought of her, was she still thinking of him? It was with this sobering thought that he walked back to Red Shirt's tepee. They'd kept his blanket for him in spite of the fact that two families shared the space. There was a quiet comfort there with the wife Chumani, the children that now smiled shyly at him as a friend. It allows him to breathe. They feed him. He feels better, he asks about their names, he knows from the Lakota boys he rode with that they all have meanings. He's told they have many names, a spirit name, an honor name, a birth name – some are secret, known only to the medicine man but then there's the nicknames – Chumani means dewdrop. The kids are Chaska and Wachiwi - eldest son and dancing girl. 'Then what would I be? *The man who don't belong?'* They don't laugh which he finds disconcerting.

It's a fine evening so he's able to sit out by the campfire with Red Shirt. He asks him if he's been to Paris yet as they are some distance from the city. Yes he has - they were all taken on a tour to see the new tower and the many fine buildings. *But has he tasted its delights?* The man shakes his head, he knows what he's referring to and the Oglalas don't go there, have nothing to do with whores, their nagi wouldn't like it. Irwin is intrigued, it's a word he keeps hearing – what is this 'nagi?' Red Shirt explains that everyone has a guiding spirit – Irwin needs to find his and that will guide him home. The mention of home silences them both. Red Shirt pokes the fire sending a shower of sparks upwards into the night. There's laughter coming from one of the other camps and as they sit they can hear, far off, someone singing 'Shenandoah'. That gets to Irwin. He tries to work out what it all means – there he is sitting in the camp of the Oglala Sioux, being told he's lost his guiding spirit and in his head he's hearing his father singing the song – when did his father ever sing? *And what's the poor man doing now?* He's floating between so many different times here; different worlds, and sitting here in this vast camp it's like it's all part somehow of the same crazy show.

Eventually Irwin breaks the silence. 'I think you're wrong sir.' Red Shirt looks at him, the fire lighting his face like a mask. 'Suppose there ain't no home anymore? For millions of folk… If there ain't no home you're wrong to tell people go look for it. '

'I didn't say it was a place. It's more than place, it's your language, customs, your dances, the stories you tell, and those stories are in the earth and the sky – but more than ever in the land walked by your ancestors for all time and where their spirits still walk. You lose the way to all that then you have no home.'

'So what of the German, the Irish, all these guys here?'

'They have to find their nagi too and you don't find it in a bottle or a French whore.'

Silence again. He envies the man's certainty, he reminds him of his mother and her faith in the Lord – and where did that get her? In this modern world the man just doesn't make sense. His grandfather had had to leave his home, what if he, Irwin, was on another journey now – if he was to stay in this country with Jacqueline, for example? He asks Red Shirt the question. He thinks about it. 'Could you then live with what you have done to your family?'

That wasn't the answer he wanted to hear.

'You have lost your nagi my son and I don't have to tell you that. You know that, I saw it in your eyes when your spirit broke free of your body.'

'That was just something I ate!' Another long silence then, 'Truth is I can't go home. They say I need a passport and I don't have one, so there.'

'Nor do I.'

'Then how you get here?'

'The show – we are like the buffalo, the horses...'

'But you got a passport?'

'Not allowed passport, not allowed citizen. We are nothing.'

'Hell's Oats Red Shirt! What do you mean you're nothing? *You are America* – who's the most popular act in the show – who does everyone come here to see? It's you! You telling me you're nothing? I seen pictures of your people with the president!'

'Pictures tell many lies. Your people tell many lies. Our elders they tell us not to do this – to have no part of this show. This show is lies.'

'Then why you do it?'

'You know why. I tell you.'

'Well there you go! You see we got something in common after all; no passport! What sort of world they making out there? If you ain't free to go nowhere? Not free in your own land – even the prairies strung with barbed wire! You're not free to leave, not free to go home. Maybe you and I we goin' to be stuck in this goddamn show of lies forever.'

*****

Another day. The band are already playing as half a dozen of the cavalry stumble into the stables and race to prepare their horses. Others are already mounted and urging their comrades on. There's a lot of cussing and angry shouting about missing the parade. One of them sees Irwin standing at the other end of the stables and calls him over, 'Don't just stand there, help us out here boy!'

He goes over and can smell the stale boose and see the bloodshot eyes. One of them sits on the hay and tells Irwin to fix his saddle. He takes out a bottle and knocks back the contents. His mate berates him, 'For fuck's sake Jess, we're missing the parade!'

'I'll catch y'up.'

A load more cursing and the rest of the cavalry head off to take their place in the grand procession. Irwin tells Jess his horse is ready for him. The man tries to swig from the empty bottle, tries to get up, he can't. He closes his eyes and collapses back into the hay. Irwin watches but doesn't try to revive him. When it's clear the man is out cold, Irwin calmly takes the man's rifle and quietly mounts his horse and heads on out.

He has a plan. His heart is pounding as he approaches the show ring. He can hear the announcer's megaphone voice echoing round the arena as he introduces the various groups and acts. He knows the rough layout of the show. He hangs back, watching the initial parade exiting the ring then regrouping for their coming scenes. It's the attack on a settlers' cabin he's waiting for. He knows how it works. First the announcer tells the story of the brave settlers and the struggle to survive the harsh life on the frontier, then the Sioux warriors charge into the ring screaming and Irwin hears the announcer's shout, 'Oh No! What's this? This poor family is being attacked by savages! The redskins are on the roof! What will happen to these poor people?'

At that point Irwin urges his horse forward and he rides into the holding area where the Cavalry are awaiting their cue. Trumpets sound, the announcer shouts 'What's this I hear?' And the cavalry charge into the ring with Irwin bringing up the rear. The cavalry circle the cabin shooting at the Indians who fall dead one by one, while the mother cowers by the wall shielding her children. One of the Indians is running away, Irwin gives chase, feet out of the stirrups, he rides, standing full height for a moment on the saddle, before crouching and launching himself at the

Indian, who shouts out in shock as they crash to the ground, 'What you doing?'

'Killing you ain't I?'

'Shooting me in the back!'

'Sorry!'

Irwin does a mock throttling, then leaps up and chases after his horse, throws himself into the saddle and joins the rest of the troupe as they do a victory circle of the ring. Meanwhile Cody has watched the whole episode with alarm. 'Who the hell? What the hell… And why ain't he wearing a uniform?'

The rest of the cavalry are similarly curious as they leave the ring. Irwin explains that he was standing in for Jess. 'You done good!' One of them says, others think the boss will be very angry, 'He won't take kind to that - you should at least be wearing the uniform.'

'Maybe I was a scout…'

Some of them see the funny side and privately Irwin is feeling mighty proud of himself. That was the biggest buzz and he can still hear the audience cheer that went up when he took down the last savage. He's warned that Jess won't thank him for what he's done. 'Why not I've saved his skin ain't I? The man was out cold with the drink.'

He's not out cold now and is on his feet, waiting when they get back to the stables. He asks the others what's going on. They explain and he looks menacingly in Irwin's direction. It's an alcoholic's blind rage that Irwin sees coming unsteadily towards him. The man growls rather than speaks, 'If you cost me boy…'

'I covered for you sir, you were out cold.'

'If you cost me dear…'

Irwin is relying on the others to come to his aid but they don't move. Jess comes nose to nose so Irwin's caught in the cloud of his stinking stale-boose breath. The man's hand grips his throat…

'Jess!'

He turns and is knocked to the floor by the gloved fist of Mr. Keen, his boss.

'You've been warned Jess, you're through. Go pack your bags you're going home.'

He then turns to Irwin, asks him his name and tells him that the colonel would like to see him.

He's feeling taller now as he walks down the row of fancy tents and under the buffalo-head entrance to the great man's tent. Mr Keen was not a man to smile but Irwin could tell things were heading in a positive direction. He's warned not to make the mistake he's just made and call it a 'show' – you can be sacked for that – it's the complete Wild West *Experience*. So he's not going to be sacked? All good so far! Inside he's offered a drink, for which he is extremely grateful, his mouth being dry as a nun's crotch. The colonel; Pahaska, or Long Hair as Red Shirt calls him, looks tired – as you would if you were running the world and playing God at the same time, but he has the gait of a showman. He and Irwin were about the same height, both done loads of crazy things in their youth - hunted most things that moved, tried their hand at trapping, prospected for gold. Story was the colonel had also driven a wagon train and ridden for the pony express. As he watches him signing programmes and making polite conversation with wealthy looking guests, Irwin likes this man and can see himself playing a similar role down the line. He identified with him – they were both triers – try anything! And here he was sitting in the man's tent - the tent of the greatest showman on earth. *I could do this!*

Mr. Keen did all the explaining - how Jess had not heeded his earlier warnings and had had to be dismissed. Irwin apologises for not having a uniform 'I was only trying to help you out sir, I love the… *experience*, you see?'

Cody was impressed with his flying dive from the horse which Irwin attributes to the time he spent with some Lakota boys. He also explains why he came to France and how it all went wrong when he was robbed of his money. The colonel is impressed – Irwin tells it in a way that anyone would be impressed! The great man gets up and puts out his hand, 'Well Mr Gurd, you got yourself a job; looks like you just joined the cavalry and good luck to you in all your endeavours. After this we go south to Marseille and you're welcome to join us.'

Irwin emerges from the tent wanting to scream! He wants to tell his family, wants to tell Jacqueline, wants to tell the whole world, '*I've done it! I'm in the Wild West Show!*' All he can do is run and find Red Shirt and tell the whole Indian camp.

The next morning he rehearses with Mr. Keen and reluctant members of the cavalry. The two who were Jess's drinking buddies are the most hostile and blank him completely. The others simply resent been called out to work in the morning. Jess apparently was a war veteran and a chronic alcoholic. Losing this job could see him on the streets but Mr. Keen assures Irwin that he had given the man many chances. At night he now has to bunk in with the men. He keeps quiet when they talk disparagingly about the savages, or say what they plan to do if they can get their hands on one particularly beautiful young squaw. He feels uncomfortable, but knows better than to open his mouth. Some of them notice his silence and don't like it - see that as a threat somehow – like you're either with us or you're against us. Is that a military thing? Some of these men have been together in real battles. You drink as one and you think as one. Irwin drinks but feels apart.

Once it's showtime all that is gone from his mind, he puts the uniform on and he charges out – at one with the troupe. That's when he can hold his own and feel proud and alive. In the mornings he practises his trick riding with Blanche, hoping he can become a solo act in the show. It's when he's happiest and he realises that's when he's always been happiest, just him and the horses. Everything else is complicated, the men, the women, even Jacqueline, that's complicated – all the women in his life, it's always been complicated, unless you pay for it. Which he can do - now he's got a job - first proper job he's had in his life where he's going to get paid regular. They're in Paris for six months then they move on, some of the men have been with the show for years – he can send money home, it's a trade, a good trade, best he's ever had. He thanks his mother and asks her to look after the family, save them from the bank. He writes his first letter home.

The men don't mind him doing that – that's allowed. Homesick is allowed. Have a drink, sing a sentimental song. Have another drink. 'We've got ourselves a day off coming up – come to Paris, buy yourself a nice little woman.' *What was it Red Shirt said? I can't remember.*

The attack on the Deadwood stage is one of the highlights for the thousands who flocked to see the show. The coach, pulled by half a dozen horses, is driven at speed round and round the arena before thirty Sioux warriors come hurtling, screaming and whooping into the ring, bows drawn, attempting to circle the coach. The drivers sitting on the box seat whip the horses on, while on the roof men start firing at the attackers. As bodies start to fall dead on both sides and the coach is brought to a halt, Buffalo Bill comes charging in on his white horse at the head of the cavalry with all guns blazing. Irwin is in the thick of it, firing in all directions until the attackers are killed or driven off. Cody then rides up and opens the door of the coach and releases the grateful passengers. For Irwin it's special, not only because he's acting out a story every child knows from books, but because he's riding into the ring with the great man himself. It's his proudest moment ever to be there and share such applause. The passengers in the coach are usually Cody's special guests and Irwin's been told they have included presidents, princes and queens. He can't believe his luck to be in such company.

Come his third performance he's still being careful not to muck up. There's been no rain so the fifty or so horses charging round the ring throw up clouds of dust. The battle all goes without incident, Irwin noting the skill of the coach drivers as they control their team of horses in the midst of the cacophony of gunfire and the war cries of the Sioux. He and his own mount have got the measure of each other and he calms her down as the fighting ends and the dust settles. He comes alongside the coach as Cody opens the door. It's all still a novelty and Irwin likes to see what sort of special guest the boss has on board; *could it be a king?* Irwin stops breathing as Cody puts out his hand and helps Carrie Dunham from the coach. She is followed by her husband

and her two children. The announcer tells the crowd that today they are welcoming, 'A great friend of France all the way from Illinois; the world's largest importer and breeder of Percheron horses, Mr. Mark Dunham!' A ripple of applause as Dunham raises his hand to the crowd then in the momentary pause that follows a child's voice calls out, 'Heh, it's Mr Gurd!' Eyes turn and suddenly everyone around the coach is looking at Irwin. He doesn't know what to do so he does nothing. He sees Carrie mouth his name. Normally he'd tip his hat to her but he's trapped in character, paralysed and wanting to be swallowed up by the earth. The announcer's talking but Irwin doesn't hear the words, aware of nothing until the band strikes up and his horse joins the rest of the troupe in leading him out of the arena.

He's so proud of what he's achieved here, but the Dunham's appearance has crushed him – he'd arrived in the Perche as a bona-fide horse trader, sat with them at the top table, held his own in the company of the most respected breeders in the world and here he was a bit-part player in a circus! More painful than that was the anger it brought back – just when he was putting the injustice behind him. How dare they come here! The very people that had driven him out!

He's removing the saddle from his horse when he hears a familiar voice behind him. It's Charles. 'Well done Irwin! That was so exciting! The family were terrified! It was so like the real thing!'

He wants to hit him, *what would he know?* He takes a breath, 'You spoke to the Indians?'

'No.'

'You should – they might see it different. It's a sham.'

'I believed it!'

Charles loiters while Irwin finishes stabling the horse, waiting, hoping Irwin will look at him. He tells him that Mrs Dunham was hoping he'd come and say hello and sign the children's programmes. The request is met with excuses; he's too busy and they have another show to do. Charles won't take a hint – he's been sent on an errand and knows he should complete his task. Irwin asks after Jacqueline and is told she was taken to the convent. Charles's platitudes about how sad it is remind Irwin what a shallow jerk the man is. He's about to walk away when he sees Carrie coming towards him with the children. There's a pulse of anger, but the kids… something tells him not to disappoint the kids. They are holding out their programmes which he signs for them. 'You never told us you were a real soldier.' Irwin could disillusion the boy but Belle saves him the trouble, 'When you coming back?'

'I'm not coming back.'

'You gotta come back – buy your horses, like Papa.'

Irwin has seen Annie Oakley handing her horse over to one of the stable lads. He points her out to the kids and tells them to go over and get her name on the programme. 'She's the one you want, not me.'

They're too shy. Carrie asks Charles to go with them. Irwin goes back to checking over his horse, which doesn't need checking over at all. Carrie watches him. The awkwardness becomes too uncomfortable, he turns to look at her. She puts her hand under his chin to stop him looking away. She holds his gaze. 'I should not have been surprised Irwin, seeing you today, I've lain awake at night wondering where you'd go, what you'd do – of course this is where you'd come.'

'Not at all. I could'a died, damn near did.'

'I've had time to consider; could a man who 'gentles' horses do what you were supposed to have done?'

'I've had time to consider too Mrs. Dunham – would I believe me if I was you?'

'I do believe you.'

'Too late now.'

'The tragedy is, I don't think anyone at the hotel really believed you doped those horses, but… a solution was needed.'

'That's what I am then – a solution?'

'Irwin, please…' she now takes his face in both her hands, it's too much but he's helpless. This is the power of the beautiful and the privileged. The kindness in her eyes could melt ice. He's not felt love like this since... All he can feel is yearning.

'Jacqueline… any word? Charles said she's in the convent.'

She now takes his hand, 'We have known Jacqueline since the first time we came over. We have seen her grow in to a fine young woman. She speaks the best English in the hotel. We were as horrified as you when we heard her fate. It's barbaric. And you've seen the cousin...'

'He's an animal.'

'Yet they say she's too bright for her own good – would they say that about a man? No they would not. The good news is that she's not locked up anymore. As soon as they knew you had left town the uncle took her back. She's not back at the hotel but I believe they needed her on the farm. It's a terrible, terrible tragedy, but Irwin, it's not our country - we can't interfere.'

He's thinking *why not?* as she takes an envelope from her velvet purse and presses it into Irwin's hand, 'Here... have you been to the Great Exhibition – by the tower?' He shakes his head. 'It's huge and spectacular – if not quite as popular as this here. It took so long to see everything there was no time left for the rest of Paris. I normally buy a number of gowns... not this year...'

Irwin holds up the envelope. 'So? You want me to go visit an exhibition? Buy clothes?'

'It's an open cheque Mr. Gurd, I will sign it and you can purchase the stallion you came here to buy.'

He forces it back into her hand, 'I don't do charity, never have, never will.'

'Don't please! Irwin when I first met you you had more life in your eyes than any man I had ever met...'

'Maybe you only ever met your husb...' Irwin stops himself and shouts out, 'Arghh! What is happening to me! Forgive me – Mr. Dunham is a gentleman! A good man and you Ma'am are an angel.'

'And you too are a good man whose reputation has been much maligned.'

He paces up and down, in turmoil once again. She stands in his way forcing him to stop and look at her, their faces inches apart. She leans even closer.

'Do you know what my mother used to say to me?'

He can only stare at her, totally beguiled. 'She said if you lose something, you don't get angry, you don't cry about it, you go back, you retrace your steps, and start looking in the place where you lost it.'

He shakes his head.

'You lost something ma'am?'

She puts the envelope back into the velvet purse, then pushes it forcefully into his chest making him step back. Eventually he takes it.

She kisses her two fingers and places the kiss on his cheek. 'Au revoir Mr Gurd, I'll see you in Nogent.'

The evening show goes by in a blur, when it comes to the finale, the Battle of Little Bighorn – Custer's Last Stand, or the Battle of the Greasy Grass as Red Shirt insisted on calling it, Irwin falls dead on cue and lies there, head in the dust, knowing that's the last time he will die. He watches the Indians whooping and circling. Somewhere out of vision Cody is still standing, firing, killing, until the ammunition runs out and the announcer lets out a dramatic 'No!!' Irwin smiles as he sees Red Shirt raise his rifle and take one last shot. 'Well… I guess that's the end of that.' he says to the other men lying dead around him.

TWELVE

The convent had been only too pleased to get rid of their troublemaking ward. On her first morning she had been presented with her dress turned inside out – the rough cloth of the outside being worn against the skin was one of the milder punishments – or forms of penance as the sisters called it. It was to act as a reminder of the pledge of obedience she had made on entering. She made no complaint. She had noticed one or two other girls suffering a similar fate and she was proud to join their ranks. The highlight of that day had been a mini riot. The girls had convinced one of their number that her father, whom she believed to be dead, was actually the priest who came to offer confession. There was a very good facial resemblance, but that was the only basis for the girls' mischievous suggestion. It would have therefore come to nothing if the girl hadn't been suddenly denied access to the confessional when he was there. This convinced everyone that he really was her father and unfortunately sent the girl a bit crazy. When she was dragged from the work room screaming 'Je veux voir mon père!' *I want to see my father!* some of the girls protested and Jacqueline, for whom such brutality was new, had taken the lead. She was happy to physically stand in the way and fight with others to free the poor girl from the sadistic nuns. The dispute inevitably culminated in the appearance of the Reverend Mother. Jacqueline, far from being cowed, demanded to know what the girl had done wrong and dared to ask why they won't let her see the priest to make her confession. Of course there is no answer other than that old chestnut, the vow of obedience. Jacqueline was warned that if she started fomenting discord amongst the girls then 'just severity' would be used against her. This she learnt from the others meant that she would be locked in a cell – solitary confinement was the Reverend Mother's favourite weapon.

When she was summoned the next day to see the woman she was therefore expecting the worst and was surprised to be met by her uncle's benign smile. The giant wimple was not even there. Another nun had offered her her clothes, told her to change, and in no time at all she was on her way out. It had been very confusing to be walking through that front door so soon. She had hardly dared to be as relieved as she felt. Her uncle had said little, he'd been beaten down over the years and knew to keep his thoughts to himself. All he would say was, 'There's work needs doing. You're no help locked up in there.' She assumed Gaston didn't want to pay, but it was still strange. She had thought of Irwin, but dared not mention his name. After a while she had asked if she could go back to the hotel. The uncle had shaken his head. 'But the money – I make money for the family…' He shook his head again. She'd asked no more questions but found the whole thing didn't quite make sense.

*****

Blanche had been in the care of the Oglala children in the Indian camp. She had refused to go anywhere near the stables, maybe they stirred bad memories – how long had she languished unwanted in the gloom of her Nogent stall before Irwin came along? Now Irwin's in a hurry to saddle her up. When stabling his other horse he'd filled his pockets with turnips, preparing for a long ride. Red Shirt and the family stand watching. Irwin makes final adjustments to the straps then gives the big man a massive hug, 'You saved my life! I'll never forget you.'

'You're going home.'

'Wherever that may be.' Irwin taps his head, 'I'm being told, I gotta do it. Think it's my ma.'

'May your nagi guide you.'

'Whatever – I gotta go!' He looks around nervously. He's still in his uniform and aware that he's about to do a runner. He makes his way swiftly round the family thanking them all, especially Chumani, who had nursed him back to life. She gives him some dried meat, telling him to stay away from berries. He thanks her yet again for what she's done for him and mounts his horse.

'You ride at night?'

'Why not – it's a good moon? Thank Pahaska Cody for me will you? I'll maybe see yous all back in Kansas!'

With that he trots off quietly through the camp, savouring for one last time the sound of a campfire fiddler.

It's not a race, he's sure the Dunhams will have travelled by train, but the fact that Mrs. Dunham had had to sacrifice her shopping excursion suggested that the horse fair must be imminent. He'll get there; moonlit nights offer up only good feelings spawned by magic times riding the great plains - away from the world, knowing the world sleeps, keeping trouble at bay. You and your equine friend calmly eating up the miles, not too fast, not too slow. It's good. It's always a good time to think, but time can still play its tricks. So much has happened in so short a time that it's now the more recent past that seems so far away. Irwin tries to pin things down – the farmer with the favoured stallion was Caillard, did the horse have a name? He can't remember… He's sure they have a deal and now, with an open cheque, he can buy it, no problem. Then what? Now it could happen, it all feels abstract, difficult to make real. Did he really run off for this, for one horse? Was that the idea? It's unnerving when your past doesn't feel wholly a part of you.

What's much more immediate as he thinks where he's heading, is the presence of Gaston, that provokes instant anger, that's real, there's no mistaking it and the thought now of seeing him at the horse fair is both good and bad. It's the scale of the injustice, the unfinished business that now boils up inside him once again. The last thing Carrie Dunham had intended was for Irwin to settle scores, but how can he not? What's happened to the gold? Will the scumbag use it at the fair? Find some unscrupulous American who will change it for francs, no questions asked? Or is it already melted down? His breathing quickens. That's real alright, that's palpable. He knows he mustn't let it get to him. He thinks of Red Shirt; what would he do? Irwin had been going to ask him why the Lakota never mined the gold themselves, only fighting to the death to get the prospectors off their land. Did they think it wrong to take from the earth? It can't be - and gold can't be the demon, the demon had been in him, when he took it from under his father's nose, as it had been in those who would kill the Indians to take it from their land, as it was in Gaston. Don't blame the gold.

The other thing that's real to Irwin as they enter the early hours of a new day, is Jacqueline; he's heading back to a lover. He can still feel exactly how he felt the first time she spoke to him, *'You are wrong! You want to know the horse, you look in the eye.'* Her voice, he plays it in his head over and over like a love song. *'Irwin...'* The way she said his name. It's like she's calling him. He can taste the first kiss and above all else can feel what it was like when she looked into his eyes and all those feelings they still consume him. How crazy is that? More than horses, more than stolen gold, it's Jacqueline; he has to admit that that's the magnet that he can feel pulling him along the road. And somehow he knows that's not the way it needs to be, that that is the most dangerous thing. He can't go down that road...

'Home' he has to think 'home' – he tries to remember what Red Shirt had told him – *it wasn't a place,* or, *it was more than just a place...* He's forgotten but knows what it means for him – he has to go back to Kansas with horses, to face his family. Hopefully it won't be too late and he can put things right. Only then will he, as Red Shirt would say, have found his nagi. His guiding spirit will have led him home. Simple... nagi, nagi, nagi - he has a plan!

*****

Jacqueline, in spite of the nagging sense of foreboding, has to admit that there is a joy in being free. Fresh air for a start, the warmth of the sun, a warm breeze. The simple idea that life can be good; that you are allowed to be elated by a summer morning. Life doesn't have to be a time of suffering, lived in perpetual fear of purgatory, of hell and of never being good enough to make it to heaven. That idea that this life should not be enjoyed, that we were all born sinners, all wretched in the eyes of God, it had permeated not only the air but the very walls of the convent. It was crystal clear to Jacqueline that the greatest sin was denial of the joy of life – down that road lay evil and within those walls it had been all around her. It was the first time she was conscious of what evil was. They created it in there. She had seen its power in the eyes of some of the girls, heard it in their desperate mumbling of the catechism and magnified many times by the ones that cried out in the night. She'd smelt it in the sour breath of the sisters and felt the envy in their eyes as they watched her leave. However she'd also loved the resistance, the spirit of those who refused to believe, not in God necessarily but in the tyranny of those whose only delight was crushing the human spirit. She only had to look around and she knew the ones that had succumbed. More alive were those girls who'd seen life on the streets, serviced men in alleyways, they were not going to be lectured by virgins who would never know anything of the world any more than they were going to make a sincere confession – much more fun to make up a lurid fantasy for the dirty old man on the other side of the grill. In that very short time she'd come to love those who refused to be afraid. She was with them and the place had lit a fire inside her, she'd been spoiling for a fight and then...

Now she was home on the farm and taking stock - thinking it all over as she worked through the million chores the family vengefully pushed her way. She realised that she'd been lucky because at worst she would only have been there a couple of years, hers wasn't a life sentence like some of the poor wretches. That end date would have allowed the battle which she now feels cheated out of. It's a frustration that the mighty wimple had got away with it. How cowardly to let her go! The strangest feeling that gnaws at Jacqueline now is that her new fate is somehow worse. How can she feel more hopeless now than she did when she was locked up? It's simple; this is the life sentence and something she can't fight against. She'll never be allowed to work at the hotel again and she will be forced to marry Gaston, that's what was written down all those years ago, so that, she has been told, is the way it will be.

It stifles Jacqueline as the day wears on. In the past she had always had a dream, something everyone around her believed was no more than a fantasy, but Irwin's arrival had promised to make it real. Not anymore. The first thing Gaston delighted in telling her when she got back was that her lover had been sent back to America. She would never see him again! That was the news that was sucking the life out of her. She'd never felt so alone. At least in the convent she had allies. Here everyone was against her and 'everyone' meant the whole of Nogent; the whole world, because Nogent was her whole world and that's the way it had always been here and who was she to dare to question it?

She stayed working outside as long as she could. Without the possibility of Irwin in her life, coming back to the brutal reality of the place was overwhelming. The family didn't even live in a proper house – their house was burnt down by a chimney fire and they had converted part of the barn. Most people, if only out of sheer necessity, rise above tragedy, but Monsieur Coqueau, Jacqueline's uncle, was not one of them. The loss of his brother, Jacqueline's father, followed by the loss of his house and the death of his favoured brood mare, had convinced him he was cursed. It was not uncommon amongst poor people. Many felt at the mercy of fate and it had sapped the pride out of him, *What was the point?* With help he could have been dragged out of it, rebuilt the house but when your son is a drunkard and a bully who has no intention of rebuilding anything, then that again defeats you. Gaston wouldn't lift a finger because he knew that half a mile away, on Jacqueline's family's land, there was a perfectly good house waiting for him. They could be in it now but they'd had to rent it out after a bad harvest several years earlier. In the meantime he was happy for them all to live in a hovel. It's surprising what you can get used to. It was only being away from it for that brief period that makes Jacqueline realise just how stark and filthy the place is. She's called in to wait on the men. There's a large bare brick fireplace at one end of the downstairs space, most of the floor is tiled with red clay tiles salvaged from the burnt house. There's a makeshift table and chairs, with various other salvaged pieces of furniture scattered around. A flight of open wooden stairs lead up to what would have been the hayloft. This is divided by cloth drapes into various sleeping spaces. It was to be no more than a temporary solution – over six years ago now.

Jacqueline is primed for abuse but at first they simply ignore her. Madame Coqueau has prepared the evening meal which appears to be a meat stew. As always it's the men that eat first with Jacqueline expected to serve them. There's four of them at the table including her younger brother Jean who has spent too much time with Gaston and is also against her. Then there are two other farmhands, Alain and Claude. Their conversations make her realise why they were so quick to get her out of the convent. The horse fair is the biggest event of the year for farmers selling their produce. Buyers come from all over the Perche and beyond, not only to buy horses but also other livestock and dairy produce. The family have geese, chickens and rabbits that they sell, as well as butter and cheese. They must be confident that any threat of her going to America has been quashed because they talk of her manning the stall on the day; doing something to make up for the money she would have brought in from the hotel. Gaston talks of *other business* he'll be taking care of. That could simply mean he'll be spending the day in the bar but she does wonder...

When she puts food on the table for them there is not even any acknowledgement that she has done it. She prefers abuse. She is not prepared to be a non-person. She takes her brother's plate away before he has taken a mouthful. He looks at her in amazement. She holds it for a moment then slowly puts it back down, he looks at the others, turns to her and says in English, 'Thank you!' They all laugh. He mimics her, 'Thank you Irwin!' He tells them how she's always talking English to herself, practising for when she goes to America. It becomes a big joke with Gaston asking who the hell would take her to America, a stupid peasant girl! That does it, she fires back – 'Not as stupid as you – at least I can write my name!' Her aunt hits her with the ladle which really gets her going, 'And do you think that doping the horses would make me want to marry you? I'd rather die!' It goes quiet and everyone stops eating. She expects the worst but then Gaston laughs, 'ce n'était pas moi – tu as le mauvais homme!' *It wasn't me! You've got the wrong man.* The men share a knowing laugh and go back to eating and drinking.

When later Jacqueline comes in from feeding slops to the pigs, her heart dips to a new low. Madame Coqueau is standing there with a long black dress. She knows exactly what it is, it's her mother's wedding dress. Her aunt tells her to put it on. It's a dilemma. She asks why, when she's not due to be married for another two years? Gaston is there with a smug drunken smile. She knows his game – he wants to show her he's won. He thinks he's being nice, speaking softly, telling her all the problems they had were her fault. *He wants to be nice to her*, fighting is no way for couples to go on. How will they have children – will he have to force her? Maybe now she'll stop being so awful to him. It's her fault he gets mad – she makes him mad! This is a new start. He urges her to put it on - this is the future, their future together. She holds the dress, sadness for her mother's stolen life overcoming all other feelings. She buries her face in the cloth longing for contact, a scent, a message of hope, for a way out other than joining her, which, at this moment she longs to do. *Aid moi Maman...* Help comes; she's able to gather herself together and tell them quietly that she can't try on the dress, it would bring bad luck. Her uncle speaks for the first time, agreeing that it would be the worst thing she could do and a tremor of fear spreads through the room. The aunt takes back the dress.

THIRTEEN

Never have so many mixed emotions gone through a man's head. As he approaches Nogent Irwin is not even sure if he'll be thrown in jail. If only he could ride in with Carrie at his side - his patron saint, he could sure use her now. What if Caillard has sold the horse? What if he sees Jacqueline? Gaston? One good thing is that a fading Blanche smells home and finds a new spring in her step. Her confident canter spurs him on as they head into town. At least he knows he's arrived on the right day. The town is alive with people and strings of horses. For a moment he questions the wisdom of arriving in his full cavalry uniform complete with gun-belt and show guns. When people look he feels a little self-conscious but proud with it. It wasn't an oversight - he wanted the world to know what he'd achieved – he'd been in the greatest show on earth! Not even the efforts of an entire town had broken him and now he was back! He only has to follow the crowd to reach the showground. It's chaotic at the entrance with people, horses and carriages all jostling for space. The scale of the event is a little daunting, it stretches ahead of him as far as he can see. Irwin has never seen so many heavy horses. They call to each other as they arrive. Blanche is a little skittish and has to be calmed down, she's in no mood for a lover! The size of the military presence is also a surprise until Irwin remembers Dunham telling him that the army was their main competitor. They run the national stud, the Haras du Pin and were determined that they should have the best bloodstock in the world. He starts to see competition stallions, standing head and shoulders above the mares, their manes and tails plaited with coloured ribbons ready for the showring. He stops to get his bearings. All round the edge of the first field there's a rope line and behind the line the sellers are setting out their stalls, unloading livestock and produce from mule carts. Looking across at another selling line, there are all manner of tethered horses, donkeys and mules. He dismounts, poor Blanche is all played out, he follows her to where she's spotted water and hay. While she eats he scans the crowds. The police chief is the first person he recognises. He passes right by him but is too preoccupied with his own dress uniform to see through Irwin's. There's no sign of Caillard or Valmy along the line. He concludes that there must be another area for competition stock. First he needs food. Blanche is reluctant to move. He can't blame her, many a wind-blown nag would not have lasted the journey one way, let alone brought him back. He ties her to a rail and makes his way across to the produce sellers. Here there's every type of poultry stuffed into crates, some open, some with the animals' heads sticking out through the grills. Then there's the cheese vendors, some with a few small cheeses in a basket on the grass, tended by a child, others selling a whole selection off a make-shift table, with girls in traditional dress and fancy lace caps. One bent old lady in black is sitting with only a few jars of pickles, a loaf and a couple of bunches of flowers she's picked from her garden. Irwin's heart goes out to her. He takes the velvet purse from his breast pocket. He opens it as he's done many times - needing to know that the cheque was real and still there, but also, intentionally or not, Carrie had left him a load of French coins – nothing to her maybe, but a few good meals for Irwin. He can still feel the thump of it on his chest, *Take it you stubborn man!* He smiles at the memory. He stops smiling, aware of someone staring at him further down the line. And there she is... Jacqueline... The moment he takes a step towards her she turns away. He understands. He saw the same fear that first time at the farm. He waits and watches, moves to where he can better see through the crowds. She's gone back to their cart and there he is – Gaston, unloading a crate of geese. She's talking to him in what looks like a normal conversation. Irwin takes a deep breath. When half the world is made up of women, how can *one* make him feel this way? And seeing her with another man... It's seeing her *talking* to the man, why is she doing that? She doesn't have to talk to him, she's supposed to hate him! Thoughts of doing harm are coming to him. In the past, back home, he dismissed any such feeling, insisted everyone was free to be with whoever they wanted. It suited him back then, but here and now, now it chokes him, burning up inside him, rooting him to the spot, but what can he do? At this moment he can do nothing except stand and stare.

He becomes aware of someone talking to him, '7th?'

He snaps out of it. 'What's that?'

'You 7th cavalry?'

It's a middle-aged American, complete with Stetson, he had spotted the uniform.

Irwin mumbles, 'Bill Cody, Wild West...'

The man looks cheated, 'You had me fooled there!' and he starts to tell Irwin his war record. It's the last thing he needs and he extricates himself at the first opportunity. He has seen Gaston walking away from the line. He makes his way over towards their pitch, holding back while Jacqueline sells a cockerel. The assurance with which she handles it, removing it easily from the crate, then taking it by the legs and hanging it upside down with one hand, as she takes the man's money with the other - it makes him want her even more. A proper farm girl, they're made for each other. He knows she knows he's there, but she doesn't look at him. He moves in closer, then right up to the line so she can't avoid him. It's some time before she speaks. 'A soldier now?'

'You know me – always pretending to be something I ain't.'

And she looks at him, 'I never thought I see you again.'

'Well here I am! I got unfinished business, you know that…' Some way behind her he sees Madame Coqueau hobbling towards their cart carrying a pail of water. '…but I don't mean you no trouble.' He touches her hand, she grabs it, every hopeless feeling she had for him coming back to her. He has to prise it lose, 'Not now… not yet…'

He turns away before the crone can recognise him. He buys a stick of bread from another stall. The two keep looking at each other from a distance as Irwin eats, then he makes himself walk off. *Home!* He repeats the mantra. He knows what it means, Red Shirt's with him now; he must concentrate on buying horses. That's all that matters, forget revenge, stop torturing yourself, forget impossible dreams, *You must go home and make things right.*

He heads for the show ring. Horses are already being trotted round under the watchful eye of military judges. They pick out the ones they favour and the rest leave, then they take a closer look and the number is further reduced. Irwin watches for a while but they're young fillies, not what he's there for. He starts to see familiar faces; Rosa Bonheur is there with her female assistant. She is sitting at her easel. She doesn't recognise him as he takes a peek at the sketches she's making. Not one for art he's impressed as a horse emerges from the paper with a few quick strokes of the charcoal. A smartly dressed woman next to him speaks to him in French. He can only say, 'Oui, oui – you are looking at the world's greatest painter of cheval… chevaux… horses…' He moves on leaving the woman none the wiser for her brief encounter with the U.S cavalry.

Behind the main arena he can hear a chorus of horses whinnying and calling to each other, this is where he finds the thoroughbreds, the highly strung stallions, smelling competition. One or two are showing off, giving their handlers a tough time. Another huge animal finds a patch of bare ground under a tree and decides to have a roll, sending clouds of dust into the air as he wallows around on his back, legs flailing, before jumping up bucking and charging round his pen. He's having the time of his life. Irwin warms to the whole highly charged scene, longing to jump over the barrier and be in there where he truly belonged. He was never born to be a spectator, but the entrance to this area is policed by uniformed men. He recognises Tacheau, he's in there - the man that had accused him of the doping. He pulls his hat a little lower on his head; that's a complication he can do without. He moves on round the perimeter and sees Dunham watching Perriot's horses having their manes plaited. There is no sign of Carrie so he doesn't make himself known – he's not even sure if Dunham would know of his wife's generosity. And where's that Charlie – he could help? He keeps searching for Caillard, he's the one he needs to find. He scans all the horses in the enclosure, one of them should be his. He can't remember what distinguished it from all the other beautiful creatures he was seeing. It was big, it was black – but so were many of the hundred or so animals in there. Coming away he sees Valmy, but the creep is with Irwin's nemesis, Quinn, the man who above all else had probably done for him. The two were a perfect match. His uniform now feels out of place, what a gift that would be for the pompous cattleman were they to meet. He changes direction fighting a sudden wave of despair. He stops, he's walking straight towards Ellwood and his party, turning again he sees Gaston who's with his anti- American mates who'd been so hostile that night in the bar. There must be thousands of people at the fair but all the ones he doesn't want to see are heading for the one place he needs to be – the showring. One of Gaston's party is looking in his direction – because he's seen a Yankee soldier or because he's recognised Irwin? Paranoia wins and Irwin walks away. He continues looking for Caillard, still hoping to see Carrie. What if they're not there? He heads back towards Jacqueline, he needs to talk to her…

On the way there's plenty to distract him, so many things he's never seen before – there's a demonstration of horsepower with single horses moving full size tree trunks. Irwin recognises the Bavarian language of those watching; he had heard settlers back home talking the same. Here the men are in traditional lederhosen, keen to buy muscle to work their forests. It's difficult not to keep watching the skill of horse and woodsman working as a team, but he moves on. There are stalls selling every imaginable form of tack. There are working saddlers, farriers, it's a horseman's paradise, but he has to keep moving. Back in sight of the Coqueau stall he sees that Jacqueline's still there, but so is her aunt. He stands for an age, watching and waiting. Sometimes you see a girl after a break and you wonder what got your blood pumping, not so with Jacqueline… and to be so close… There are distractions, a few times passing kids are pushed forward to say 'hello' in their best English and ask if his guns are real. He can't let them down and has to do draw, spin and 'shoot'. They all seem to know the word 'cowboy' and 'peau rouge.' He keeps his eyes on the stall but it's hopeless, the aunt will not go away. Irwin gives up and makes his way back to the ring. Various horses are being led away now, their particular classes having being judged. He gets a move on, panicking, worried he may be missing out. As he comes close to the arena, there's a commotion and there in the midst of it is Caillard. He is leading his horse away from the ring pursued by just about everyone Irwin loathes. The war-wounded Valmy seems to be at the centre of a huge row. Gaston and his mates are haranguing him in French and Quinn is shouting at him in English. Caillard and his stallion look like they are trying to walk away from the lot of them. Irwin follows until they get back to Caillard's cart. He stands back, unnoticed, for a moment trying to work out what's going on. Caillard simply puts hay and water down for his horse while Gaston and his mates harangue Valmy. Quinn goes and looks over the stallion – like he's buying it? *No!* Irwin steps forward, Gaston stops mid-sentence on seeing him. They all turn. 'Afternoon gentlemen, Monsieur Valmy, Monsieur… and Mr. Quinn… What's up y'all look like you seen a ghost?' No one moves for an age. *Interesting…* Irwin's never made such an impressive entrance in his life. He starts to piece together what he thinks is going on. Gaston looks dead worried, as does Valmy. Quinn looks cocky as ever. He's the first Irwin needs to deal with. 'So… what's the tale with you Mr. Quinn?

'I'm buying me a stallion. What 'd'you think country boy?'

'I think you didn't choose that fine looking animal on your own.'

Irwin looks to Valmy, who shrugs, 'You leave town.'

'Now I'm back and sorry to disappoint you Mr. Quinn but that stallion's going home with me.'

Quinn laughs. 'I am doing the deal right now! Don't start country boy – everyone knows you ain't got two cents to your name! Where you been – shooting injuns in the Wild West Show?' He laughs again.

Irwin turns to Caillard, 'Remember me, Monsieur? Monsieur Valmy will you remind that gentleman that we shook on a deal.'

'But you was not here…'

'I am now.'

He walks over to the horse which provokes a further outburst from both Gaston and Quinn. Irwin's eyes are now on the protesting Gaston. He asks Valmy to translate. The middleman can feel the jaws of a trap closing in on him. He mutters and stutters, first in French then, 'Monsieur Coqueau - ici, he was wanting to buy this horse, mais Monsieur Quinn…'

'I outbid him, simple as that.'

Gaston gets the gist of what's going on and grabs Valmy insisting that the horse must stay in France; Valmy must work for him, not the Americans. His mates are all backing him up. It's clear to Irwin what's going on as both Gaston and Quinn vie for Valmy's services. He interrupts and suggests that the solution is for them *all* to make an offer. He takes out the velvet purse and holds it up, his eyes fixed on Gaston. 'That's my offer, Mr. Quinn?'

Quinn insists that he's already made his offer to which Irwin counters, 'Say I've just topped it?'

'How the heck do I know?'

'You say what you think the horse is worth.'

He laughs, 'Whatever's in there I'll double it.'

'Could be nothing; two times nothing is nothing. That won't do - name your figure Mr. Quinn.' He turns to Gaston, 'And you sir – I want to see the colour of your money! Tell him Valmy – his money, I want to see his money!'

Gaston asks the cornered Valmy what's going on. He explains to him that Irwin wants to see his money. At that Gaston and his two cronies make it quite clear that they are not playing that game. The horse is staying in France! Valmy tries another solution explaining to Irwin that the horse didn't in the end win Best Young Stallion, so it's not as good as he thought it was, so maybe…

Quinn will have none of it, 'The only reason he didn't win was 'cus the whole show is fixed – these kinda shows always are! That Ellwood, the barbed wire man – he wanted this horse but was talked out of it – I saw it with my own eyes – that's when I knew – this is the best damned stallion! But, what do y'know - they don't like this Mr. Caillard because he don't play along with them and sell them his colts. I take my hat off to you sir, now if we could forget this nonsense, ignore these jokers and do the deal…'

There's a click as Irwin draws and cocks his gun. Quinn instinctively raises his hands, but the barrel turns towards Gaston. Irwin holds it to his temple. A passer-by screams and someone calls for the gendarme, but Irwin remains calm, 'I said show me your money.' There's a panicked exchange between Gaston and Valmy as a crowd gathers. Valmy explains that Gaston says he doesn't have any money. Irwin smiles, 'Then how was he going to buy the horse?' Gaston points to Valmy, 'Lui, il l'a!'

'Non, non, non!' Valmy waves his arms.

Irwin now knows for certain what the game is. 'Of course he doesn't have any money – that's why he needs his middle-man, 'cus he's not bidding francs is he? How about Yankee dollars, like Gold Double Eagles?'

Quinn tries to intervene, 'Now you gone crazy, boy!'

Irwin draws the second gun and points to Valmy as the crowd start shouting to fetch the law. 'I got nothing to lose here – I'll count to three… one… two…'

'Le voici, le voici!!' and out of his leather shoulder bag the three fingered hand produces a smaller cloth sack.

Irwin gestures to Quinn, 'Can you do me the honour sir – look in the bag.'

He puts a hand in, keeping one eye on Irwin. His eyes widen as he brings out a coin, 'Oh my… well I'll be… that's gold!' He feels the weight. 'If that ain't a Double Eagle!'

'Irwin!!'

A desperate shout rings out across the showground; a woman's voice. Hearing it, Irwin momentarily drops his guard. Gaston throws himself at him sending the two of them crashing to the ground. Irwin wasn't the only one to hear his name called. Carrie Dunham was walking away from the show ring with Virginia, the children and Charles. She sees Jacqueline running across the field, 'Go Charles!'

Obedient, if not fully understanding, Charles runs after Jacqueline. They find the two men locked in a vicious fight. Jacqueline screams at them to stop. Gaston maybe shorter than Irwin but he's like a fighting dog, bred for such moments. There are fights and there are *fights*; the former when you only need to show someone not to mess with you maybe, where there are boundaries, the punch is judicious, and then there's the slaughter, where blind rage takes over and you have no control – kill or be killed. The first blows tell both men this is going to be dirty and Gaston's animal strength soon gives him the upper-hand. Jacqueline screams, begging Charles to stop them. It's a ridiculous request until he sees Irwin's gun lying on the floor. He picks it up and fires it into the air, 'Decease immediately!'

To his surprise Gaston releases his hands from Irwin's throat. The hiatus is long enough for both the military and the police to intervene and pull the men apart. A gendarme demands Charles hand over the gun. Before he can do so Irwin grabs it and points it at Gaston. Jacqueline screams again, begging Irwin to stop. He refuses; he's doing nothing until Gaston admits to doping the horses.

'But Irwin, it wasn't him – he didn't do it!'

Mayhem ensues, Irwin raging, out of control, threatening all and sundry with the gun. The police and the military are both in turn threatening him, while Jacqueline is yelling at Gaston to tell the truth.

Alain, his crony, steps forward and pokes Irwin on the arm, 'C'était moi.'

All the shouting stops. Irwin lowers the gun, 'You? You doped the horses?'

Alain addresses the crowd telling them that the horses weren't harmed. He did what he had to do. He asks how else could they preserve what was theirs, what belonged to the Perche, to France?

By now the chief of police has arrived and recognising Irwin, assumes he's the troublemaker and demands his men disarm and arrest him, but Jacqueline intervenes, protesting his innocence. Chaos continues with arguments about the gold, the purchase of the horse, the double dealing Valmy. It's too much for the police chief, he has all the main protagonists carted off to the gendarmerie. As he leaves Irwin sees Carrie for the first time. She smiles at him, 'Welcome back Irwin.'

'The gold – they got my gold!'

'You know where I am if you need me.'

The children want to know what's going on. She reassures Wirth that arguments happen sometimes if two people want the same thing. Belle calls her, 'Mama, Mama, look what I've found!'

She picks up the velvet purse which has been trodden into the earth.

'Oh thank you dear – did I drop my purse?'

Jacqueline remains, alone, watching the two main men in her life being taken away. She sees Quinn talking to Caillard which only compounds her helplessness. She feels someone touch her arm and turns, it's Carrie who takes a handkerchief and wipes a tear from the poor girl's cheek. She tells her not to worry, she will send Charles to the gendarmerie and make sure Irwin is okay. Charles discreetly protests, he should even now be assisting Mr. Dunham with business and shouldn't Mrs. Dunham be there too for photographs? Carrie sighs, it's not her top priority right now. Jacqueline grips Carrie's arm, her attention has gone back to Quinn who is now leaning on the cart writing with Caillard looking on. Carrie understands, suspects she knows what's happening and goes across to them. 'Good afternoon Mr. Quinn, would you by any chance be thinking of buying a horse?'

'No, Ma'am, I have *bought* me a horse!' and he shakes Caillard by the hand. Carrie doesn't know what to say. It is none of her business and it looks like she's too late anyway. Quinn is very pleased with himself. 'You saw that ruckus just now? Well, all I can say is *money talks bullshit walks!'*

Carrie turns away, finding the man uncouth. She apologises to Jacqueline, there was nothing she could do. All she can say is that Charles will make sure Irwin comes to no more harm. She urges the girl to be careful and to look after herself then reluctantly heads back to the show ring followed by the rest of her party.

The men are in the police station for hours. Valmy is now the middle-man in more ways than one, desperately protecting his ass from all sides – he was the one who was holding the Yankee gold. He knows it's Irwin's, but Gaston denies any knowledge of it, so how did he come by it? Alain is the only one happy to tell it straight. When Irwin remembers him coming out of the dentist's tent at the fair, he admits that that was where he acquired the chloroform to dope the horses. He is proud of what he's done. The truth of the situation – the robbery of Irwin by Gaston, the framing of Irwin for the doping - it all becomes crystal clear but the police chief is damned if he's going to charge one of his own countrymen in front of this upstart Yank in fancy dress. Apart from anything else it would be admitting that he had got it wrong. He concentrates instead on reading out at length a law dating back to 1563 forbidding the carrying of weapons in public. Irwin doesn't understand a word of it but is losing patience as he senses that once again justice is not about to be done. Valmy the hapless translator struggles to mediate. It's only when Carrie appears with Charles that matters are finally resolved. Never before has such natural beauty, elegance and haute couture graced the building. The police chief is reduced, a natural subservience overtakes him, in spite of Alain's disgusted gaze. A speedy resolution is the only way to save face. Irwin is reunited with his gold - and the guns, that Charles assures the man are show guns and only fire blanks.

Emerging from the building Irwin is pumping, desperate to find Caillard. Carrie has to tell him the bad news – Quinn has bought the stallion. The bag of gold suddenly weighs a ton and Irwin feels it dragging him to the ground. He can't speak. His legs have gone, a complete exhaustion leaving his whole body powerless. Carrie and Charles ask urgent questions about his health and Carrie promises to ask her husband to help him find as many horses as he wants, 'It's not over!'

Irwin can only shake his head. After everything he's been through, after racing back, riding through a sleepless night, surviving the fight of his life, after everything the world could throw at him… and for what? Only now does he feel the punches that Gaston landed on him. His battered body starts to shake. Charles is dispatched to find water.

He meets Gaston and Alain coming out of the gendarmerie followed by Valmy. He stands aside, relieved as they hurry off in different directions. Carrie watches them go. She's not the only one - as soon as they're out of sight Jacqueline emerges cautiously from an alleyway. She leads Irwin's horse over to him. 'You forget Blanche…'

That brings Irwin to his feet. He hugs the horse, seeking some of her strength. Jacqueline asks if he's alright. He stares at her, but looks to her like he's far away. He mutters, 'What do I have to do?'

She gently wipes blood and dirt from his face. Carrie tells Jacqueline that she has told him about the horse being sold.

'I can help…'

'No one can help.'

'My uncle he has mares…'

Anger stirs again, 'I don't want mares! One stallion, that's all – I would'a settled for that!'

Jacqueline is fighting back tears. Charles brings water. Irwin rejects it. Jacqueline takes it and puts it to his lips. He drinks and spits blood from a cut in his mouth. She feeds him again. Carrie suggests that she and Charles should leave them. Before doing so she reunites him with the velvet purse and assures Irwin that she is more determined than ever to help him return home with the horses he came for. 'Tomorrow is another day and in the mean-time there will be a bed waiting for you at the hotel.'

He stares at her but can say nothing. The black cloud has engulfed him.

When they've gone Jacqueline tries to kiss the spark back into her lover. He knows that too is doomed but can't resist the warmth, the touch and the taste. He needs her now, feeling weaker than he's ever felt. He asks her again, 'What do I have to do?' She knows that she has to be the strong one. He has to listen to her and he will be alright. She makes him look her in the eye and tells him that he will go back to the hotel, he will see Sidonie and ask her to bring him at first light to the Dechanel farm. She will be there waiting for him. He has questions but Jacqueline can't stop to answer them – she is already in big trouble, her aunt will be waiting and she has to go. The farewell embrace takes them both back, reignites the fire. She has to force him to let go and she disappears into the maze of alleyways that will take her back to the showground.

Things are not that good in the Dunham bedroom. Dunham has had an excellent day and made some very satisfying deals. Now is not the time to be telling him that he was complicit in a grave miscarriage of justice. In fact the last thing he wants to hear now, as he dresses for dinner, is the name Irwin Gurd. It's personal, he can't help it, but he's seen the way she's behaved around the young man from the very first time they met. If he knew himself at all, he would have to admit that he was extremely jealous, but he is not aware that that is what is responsible for his moody silence. What grates with him is the way she persists in discussing the means by which they can help the lad. Charles has shared with Carrie everything he knows of the threat to Irwin's family back home. Even now the bank could be repossessing their farm. How can they stand by when they are in a position to help? Dunham insists his wife is being ridiculous – how can they possibly help?

'We could telegraph, at least let the family know he's alive.'

'Do you know the cost of a transatlantic telegram?'

It is indeed very expensive – a luxury enjoyed only by the wealthy, but as Carrie points out, that is exactly what they are and her husband wouldn't hesitate to send any number of business messages. Her persistence threatens to ruin their evening. In the end he agrees to instruct Charles to do whatever Carrie sees fit to help the young maverick. Harmony is restored, she always gets her way.

The last thing Irwin feels like doing is going back to the hotel, but Blanche deserves her bed and bed is all he desires too; to close his eyes and disappear from the world. As he heads back Jacqueline's instructions repeat themselves in his head, becoming a reality, but posing a massive question; what do they mean?

There's one telegraph system that appears to be cheap and efficient. By the time Irwin makes his weary way into the hotel yard word has already reached Sidonie and she's waiting for him. News in this town sure travels fast. Irwin is the talk of the staff and they now somehow regard him as one of their own. Only Fournier, the greasy lubricant between the two worlds of his fiefdom, resents his return. He'd disliked Irwin from their very first encounter; everyone should know their place, to upset the order can only cause trouble – know your history – look at the commune, look at the revolution… and now he's been instructed to have a room and a bath ready for the trouble-maker's return. Sidonie takes him up to the familiar garret on the top floor. He's not complaining but this time he won't be handing over every stitch of clothing he possesses. He's happy to hold onto his cavalry uniform, torn and bloodied from the fight, if Sidonie could please clean the screwed up suit he produces from his saddle bag.

It's the strangest feeling of déjà-vu; to be naked in this bath-tub and see the water turning red. He feels for the lump on his head. It's long since gone. He surveys the fresh bruises that are now beginning to bloom on his blemished skin. He notes where the old scabs have been newly rubbed off a grazed knee, watches the spiral of leaking blood. He sees where teeth marks have branded the back of his wrist. He shudders at the memory; it was a fight he would have lost, he knows it, but then he finds himself grinning at the absurdity of Charles firing the gun, *'Decease immediately!'* He lets the warm water once again work its magic and a new idea takes hold. With his eyes closed Carrie and his mother start to merge into one. Carrie is undoubtedly his saviour but suppose she's the reincarnation of his guardian angel, the mother who somehow guided him here against all the odds. Is his mother now working through this other vessel? Red Shirt would understand, are they his nagi? The idea warms him. And now Jacqueline was summoning him to some unknown location. She must have a plan. He pictures her there with her bag, ready, waiting to run away with him…

A knock on the door brings an exhausted Charles carrying his portable writing slope. His trip to France is turning into a nightmare. The demands from Dunham weigh heavily on his young shoulders. He and Perriot are in the midst of complex financial negotiations with them both assuming the young man has a more thorough grasp of international banking than is the case. It's a huge responsibility. What he doesn't need therefore is Mrs. Dunham instructing him to act as Irwin's agent. It's the end of a very long day. He tells Irwin that he has been assured that there's nothing to stop him buying horses even at this late stage, but he can't do it with gold double eagles – *what was he thinking?* He needs the services of a bank…

'Well the Lord works in mysterious ways his wonders to perform!'

'I beg your pardon?'

'Ain't it just the luckiest stroke that I met you Charlie?'

An hour later Charles leaves with instructions on how to contact Irwin's family, his personal details to once again arrange travel documents and most unwelcome and unnerving – the heavy bag of gold, for which he has given Irwin a signed receipt. Irwin offers up a thank you prayer to his mother, to Carrie, to the great whoever and sinks into a deep sleep.

Sidonie is waiting by the stables at first light and Blanche is saddled up in the yard. The youngest of the stable lads is already on a horse, waiting to guide him to Dechanel. Irwin asks Sidonie what Jacqueline is planning but she will only shrug as though she doesn't understand or doesn't know. She wishes him bonne chance and he sets off. It's not a long ride, at one point Irwin felt they were heading towards the dreaded family farm and is relieved when they turn off down a lane he doesn't know. Eventually the young lad stops and points to a track that you would miss if you didn't know it was there. It's just wide enough for a cart, but with grass growing in the wheel ruts, like it's not much used. It's bordered by high hedges and trees that soon form a canopy, cutting out the light. He proceeds cautiously, slightly nervous about where this tunnel is leading. For some reason he can feel his heart beating. In the gloom the morning air still has a chill, then flickering shafts of sunlight start breaking through, making the leaves shimmer. The track opens out into what he assumes to be the Dechanel farm. To make him even more uneasy, the first thing he sees is Jacqueline's uncle sitting on an old chair by the farmhouse. Hopes of a secret lover's tryst evaporate in a moment. *What's going on?* Then he sees her. She comes out of a barn, stops on seeing him, then takes a few steps in his direction, but that's it – there's no running to her lover, no embrace. In her uncle's presence she is restrained – only a nervous smile and a look in her eye give him hope – her eyes are alive like she has a plan. Irwin looks around before he dismounts. He's taking no chances after everything that's happened – *why is the uncle here? Where's Gaston?*

She introduces her uncle, Irwin reminds her they've already met. He asks what's going on and she leads him across the yard. An old woman is hanging out bedding from an upstairs window, talking to some unseen person inside. She hardly gives them a glance. They come to a field backing on to a wood. About a dozen horses are grazing, the animals turn their heads and look their way, then start to slowly wander over. Jacqueline discreetly touches Irwin's hand, 'What do you think?'

He says nothing. *Still trying to sell me mares?* With her uncle now arriving he supposes anything else would be a fantasy. He shakes his head and surveys the stock, there's not one stallion among them.

'He sell you six. The best mares in the Perche.'

'Why? Your family hate me…' and to the uncle, 'You know I'm a Yank!'

'His son robbed you.'

'The low-downest scum...'

'He wants you to know, we are not bad people.'

He looks at her, wanting her now more than any number of horses. 'Couldn't stop thinking of you, you know that, when I was gone? Couldn't help myself. Horses… sure I can buy horses, the world's full of horses, but you… there's only one of you. I'm back for you…'

'Don't Irwin! Stop!'

'That's the truth.'

'No!' She bangs her fists down on the fence, struggling now, 'I have gave my word; he sell horse to you…' she takes a breath, '… then I marry Gaston.'

'You what? Why in hell's name d'you say that?'

'So you can go home! You can not go home without the horse.'

'What if I can't go home without you?'

'Don't! Don't play games with me! You know that is what I want!'

'It's what I want too. You are the most beautiful woman I have ever met. Even your voice is music you know that? Like a love song. I never said this to a woman before, but Jacqueline I love you!'

'If you love me, you go!!'

'No! I can't let you do this!'

She shakes her head and runs off, it's all too much. Irwin knows not to follow. The uncle keeps his attention on the horses. Irwin also gives them a cursory glance but his mind is elsewhere, trying to come to terms with Jacqueline's proposal, her enormous sacrifice. He doesn't know what to do.

After a while the uncle looks at him, he looks at the uncle, they neither of them know how to proceed or even how to speak to each other. He turns on hearing someone coming from the yard. It's not Jacqueline, it's her younger brother, Jean. He is leading a small pony over to the field. As it comes near the pony becomes lively and the lad has to hold it on a tight rein. Jacqueline follows, wiping her tear-stained cheeks, her face set. She doesn't come near to Irwin. He asks her what's going on as the pony, cock growing, calls to the mares.

'Souffler mais pas jouir.'

'What?'

'We use her to say when the mares…'

'Are in season?'

'He does the work, but never have the pleasure.'

Irwin watches the pony calling and the females responding. He's trying to work out what the game is. She talks to her uncle who is pointing out various mares. She nods, takes note and tells Jean to take the pony back. She turns to Irwin, 'You see?'

'No… well yes, but no… I get it - he does the work but don't get the cherry… but that ain't me Jacqueline…'

'You are so stupide! This is not about you!' She points to Jean heading back into the stables, 'Look - that is my little brother.'

'Sure, I got me one of them too.'

'And that is why you have to go and I have to stay.' She explains that this is her parents' farm, the house rented out at the moment but when she is twenty one it will become hers and she will marry Gaston and the land will stay in the family. She will do this for her brother. 'And you, you will go back, for your family, you will go back…' She touches his arm, '…but look… you have here, you can buy mares in season… '

'So?'

'So…' Jacqueline, curses, finding the whole business upsetting, frustrated that Irwin needs her to spell out what she is offering. She goes closer to him, not giving her uncle the chance to pick up on her conversation. 'The stallion you did want…'

'That that bastard Quinn robbed me of?'

'Tais-toi! Listen to me. It is still there avec Monsieur Caillard until it goes to the train tomorrow.'

'It's where?'

'Not far, very close…' It takes a moment then he grabs Jacqueline as the penny drops, she has to shrug him off. 'You have one night.'

'Ain't you just the brightest woman in the whole of France? You help me?'

She doesn't answer but allows herself a smile and for the first time he smiles too, takes hold of her so she can't get away. He kisses her before she again pushes them apart.

'So before long I could have me a stallion after all…'

'Peut être, more than one.'

'More than one... If we put 'em together tonight?'

With that Irwin turns his attention to the mares and to the uncle. They select half a dozen that he's picked out, a price is agreed and he shakes on a deal. The fact that he's using Quinn's stallion is the best thing about the whole business; the fact that

Quinn won't know is the sweetest revenge he's ever known! He goes to punch the air but Jacqueline's watching him and it hits home just what it means; it means he's agreeing to give up any hope of her. That can't be right. He insists that he must now take her to America like he promised he would. That was their original deal, 'You help me find horses, I'll take you to America.' That was the deal, 'And you done your part…'

Now, more than ever he insists they're made for each other. She turns away from him, anger growing; she won't do it – does he understand nothing? She has given her uncle her word – maybe Irwin doesn't know what that means, maybe Americans don't keep promises... She's shouting now and her uncle is watching. Irwin stops her. He can see her pain and he can't bear it. A hopeless silent stalemate sees him wandering around, looking over the horses, taking in the farm, the uncle, wanting the man to go; desperate to be alone with Jacqueline, to talk, but she's not even looking at him. He knows, he knows what she's doing is right– right for him, it's what he should be doing, he knows it, 'Fuck!!' He will go along with her plan. If she could somehow help him introduce the stallion to his young ladies then he'll agree, he'll go back without her – 'And that'll be the hardest thing I ever done in my life…'

It's agreed he will pay in francs – cash not cheque, the next day. Charles will see to it – although he doesn't yet know it. When it comes to the deal Irwin now talks with all the confidence of a man with a bank behind him. He notices that Jacqueline is now turning her attention more to her uncle. This man never smiles, shows little outward emotion but has an overwhelming sadness in his eyes. Irwin realises that this deal must have consequences for him too. Has he broken ranks with the family? How will it go down with his own son? Jacqueline massages his hands in a loving gesture as she stares into his eyes. At least there's love between these two – he can see it. He will leave them alone, wondering what trouble he's laying in store for them. That too makes him feel bad. He makes an arrangement to meet Jacqueline by the Caillard farm. She has it all worked out. Nogent is holding a last night dance and fireworks, so everyone will head to town to celebrate. It seems too easy but she shrugs in her usual, matter of fact way. He can only trust her. It's a bitter-sweet parting. He reluctantly rides back up the track; he'd done it – he'd bought his Norman horses… but not even a kiss as he left?

Luckily Carrie is spending the last day in the hotel with the children. Without her help he would have no hope of gaining Charles's attention. The young banker had been off early with Dunham, completing deals, but Carrie corners him when he returns and is able to assure Irwin that he will have the funds he requires. What can he say? No words seem adequate. She invites him to join them for lunch eager to learn about his purchase. In the café the children soon get bored – even the thrill of sitting with someone from the Wild West Show soon wanes and Virginia takes them off to see the trains. It feels strange, Irwin's aware that there hasn't been a day like this since he arrived. A sense of ending. He's made a deal, he's bought horses and now he's sitting in a café, with the beautiful wife of the world's greatest horse dealer… and he's almost relaxed. For once he has nothing to hide. He feels that this woman knows all his failings, he doesn't have to bullshit anymore and she's actually interested in the real Irwin, the family back home, his dreams for the future. He admits that that is all he has – a dream. As he attempts to flesh it out he's aware that she keeps staring into his eyes. Part of him wants to undress her, strip away all that finery – would they then be equal? Could she be thinking the same thing? Conversation stops. He's never been lost for words but his mouth is dry and his heart is pounding. She takes his hand, 'Irwin… I think you and I share one regret…'

'*You* have a regret?'

'I do - one thing I can't help you with.'

'You helped me more than I can say Ma'am!'

'Jacqueline should be on that boat when you leave.'

'You're damned right she should.'

'But we are guests in this country…'

'You told me that before. It don't make it no easier.'

'I know and my regret is that for all you have achieved, I can see you hurting. The night I watched you dance, I remember your laughter back then. You should be laughing now…' She takes his other hand, 'I think you're in love. You haven't laughed once today, even your smile, it's not what I remember.'

'I gave the uncle my word.'

'I know. I'm sorry, you've done the right thing.'

'That's not my style.'

'I know… but believe me it will hurt less with time – we've all had love that has to be denied.'

'You?'

'Of course. Arranged marriage isn't restricted to the Olde World. You get over it I promise you – so I want to see that smile. Come to the fireworks tonight – there'll be dancing…'

'Will you dance?'

She shakes her head. 'I'll be happy to watch you.'

'Right…'

They remain looking into each other's eyes. The moment passes where, with a lesser woman, he would have made his move. Now he'll never know… He keeps looking, they are both comfortable in the silence, she still holding his hands. He wants to tell her why he won't be there this evening but he doesn't say a word. There's one last hurdle and he doesn't want to jinx it.

FOURTEEN

Caillard doesn't know he's being watched as he rides away from his farm. Irwin's surprised the man's even going to the dance - the likes of Gaston and his mates must hate him. Maybe he's finalising things with Quinn or showing the Perriots and Tacheaus that they don't control the game. Whichever way it is, he's looking proper dressed up – no old smock, but a smart looking suit and he's heading off at a sprightly trot; who knows what dreams he hopes the Yankee dollar will buy. As soon as he's out of sight Irwin nudges Blanche out from behind the hedge. Jacqueline emerges onto the track ahead of him at exactly the same time – what a team they are! She's come prepared with a halter draped over her shoulder and in no time she's done the business and is leading the horse out of the stable. She hardly speaks – this is a venture fraught with risk. Her eyes are everywhere making Irwin realise this is not the merry jape that he thought it would be. He reminds her that they're not stealing nothing – they're only borrowing…

Irwin undoes the gate to the field as Jacqueline reaches up to slip the halter from the horse's neck. The animal's already frothing at the mouth and the mares are heading over. Irwin admires the mighty beast that was nearly his. There's a pang of regret as he looks up into its eyes, strokes his mane - so long it covers the entirety of his massive neck and still wavy from being plaited for the show. All he can do now is hope… 'There you go boy, lovely ladies, they're all yours.' They watch the courting ritual as he nudges and sniffs his way from mare to mare. Some are skittish and don't want to play, others offer themselves, head bowed, calm and somehow knowing. As the beast mounts his first bride Irwin wants to hold Jacqueline, to acknowledge the moment. He can't watch without feeling connected, in touch with that most basic force in the universe, the one drive that unites everything that lives on the planet. A moment of creation. He can feel it, can't she? He looks to Jacqueline, she won't look at him, why not? She has to be feeling what's in the air here. He knows what she feels for him – how can she be so hard, so strong?

The stallion seeks out his second mate. He mounts but seems to have trouble entering. Jacqueline calmly walks over and raises the member to the correct trajectory. As she returns to the gate she smiles and shrugs. Everything this woman does makes Irwin want her even more, yet still she keeps her distance. They keep watching as the sun sets. Jacqueline wants to go but Irwin's reluctant - only three mares have been covered. She insists that's not a problem - they will leave the boy to do his job, 'He has all the night.'

'You leaving him here?'

She picks up the halter and starts walking away, Irwin follows not at all sure that they're doing the right thing, trying to foresee the consequences. She reassures him, 'I think Monsieur Caillard leave open the stable door – stupide! A stallion, he will do what he will do, yes?'

Irwin has to admire her gall, 'And in the morning?'

'Jean, he come here every morning. He see him, he will take him back. It happens… happens all the time.'

She shrugs and only stops walking when she comes to the farmyard. She turns to face Irwin, 'I go that way …' She points across the yard.

No... This could be the last time they'll be alone, Irwin is not sure how he is supposed to behave. 'Well… I guess, it's thank you Mr. Quinn – looks like I'll be going home with more than I paid for.'

'You pay for it.'

'Guess we both did…' It's awkward now, 'May I?' He moves in to kiss her. She tries to make it platonic… she tries but feels some dam within her burst, her arms fly round him, clutching him, trying to make herself disappear within his embrace. She's lost now, drowning in the flood, pulling him out of sight into the barn. Into the darkness where they both let go, let themselves be swept away, struggling, their clothes torn off them, tossed in rapids, out of control until they find themselves going nowhere, gasping for breath … finally naked together for the first time. They hold back now to discover this new world, letting themselves explore and be explored. A tenderness to savour, fingers tracing, tracing features as eyes start to see in the darkness, to feast and lips to feel. Such delicacy… until a new wave builds and they're powerless against it. They let themselves be taken, they long to be taken… She offers herself up and her cry rings out through the barn. And they are as one, as they know it was meant to be, carried as one, deep in the wave, the all engulfing force that builds and builds and has to break - it breaks and they're at one now with the stallion and the mare and the whole universe that explodes within them and all around them.

Only their breathing now disturbs the silence and gradually that subsides. Fear flashes like lightning in Jacqueline's brain, it's not articulated, not even to herself and like lightning it's gone in the moment of Irwin's kiss, but it was real, *Have we created life?* Was that what that was all about?

A woman's fear dismissed. They lie together, make love again, together trying to avoid the inevitable, to make time stand still. It gives no quarter, all too soon with the very first sign of approaching dawn the mood changes. She has to get back before sunrise, she will douche with vinegar like the girls in the convent had told her. Gaston will have been drunk at the dance so he won't be around all morning. It's only her aunt… These are the pressing matters for her. For Irwin he simply wants to know if he will see her when he collects the horses. She is scrambling to find her clothes. 'Not like this chéri!'

They manage to smile before they share the same thought, *Not like this, ever again?*

She leads him back to poor tethered Blanche. She adjusts his thrown-on cavalry jacket. 'This is how I'll remember you - my soldier…'

He takes his hat and the gun-belt from the saddlebag to complete the picture. He draws, spins and 'shoots'. 'There you go – your soldier – I'll fight for you anywhere.'

She shakes her head, 'But you can't! You can't…'

She turns away, upset.

'Why not, why not Jacqueline?

'You promise!'

'Well, I've always been of a mind that promises is there to be broken.'

'Non!'

He turns her to face him, holding her arms, 'It don't feel right, leaving you. That Gaston he don't care for you…'

She pushes herself free and runs off.

'Jacqueline! Wait!'

But the sun's coming up, she doesn't turn back. He can only watch her go. He watches until she's out of sight. He curses quietly; *how can life go to hell so fast? You didn't even say good bye…*

There's movement and a quiet snuffling in the field behind him. He looks - the stallion is there with his harem. They're *his* mares, his future. It means nothing. He can't make it mean anything. Blanche gives him a thump with her nose, a wake-up call to the new day.

Jacqueline's return home does not go unnoticed, she had stayed too long, it's daylight and her brother is up and about. He sees her slipping into the barn. He knows better than to confront her. A short time later, perhaps sooner than usual, he makes his way across the fields from one farm to the other. The horses are expecting him and come to the fence. He sees the stallion and checks the gate and the boundaries – all intact. He goes to the barn, wondering… He stops - the dirt floor is a mass of footprints. He can't help but notice - he's the only one goes in there and they're not made by his clogs. He looks around, a picture emerging. There's a halter lying in the hay - the hay is flattened, he's sure of it… and looking more closely there's blood, spots of blood.

He returns the stallion to its home. There's no sign of Caillard which is good. He leads the horse into the stable and quietly leaves. He walks back, an anger brewing, all trust in his sister gone, a threat hanging over his own future.

By the time he gets back to the hotel Irwin has pulled himself together. He's relived the wonder of the night, the best night he's had in his life. The carnal memory overrides all other emotion. He's in awe of his woman, convinced that somehow they will be together. He'll save her, there's still time, he will not leave without her! Before that there's business to complete and the idea that he could be taking home pregnant mares, that he could have colts sired by the foremost stallion in the Perche… He's on cloud nine and it's all down to the genius of his lover!

He hands the horse over to the lads in the yard, 'You take care of her now – she's coming home with me.' He goes in to find Charles; today's the day everything has to be paid for and for once in his life he's confident that the bank of Carrie will see him okay.

As soon as he walks into the lobby he hears clapping coming from the dining room, then the unmistakeable measured tone of Dunham. He stands in the hallway listening.

'The only way we can accommodate the number of animals is to lay on special trains to Le Havre, which I have arranged.' Someone asks how many horses they're talking about. Dunham answers, 'More than ever before, gentleman. This year we will, between us, be taking over three thousand horses, a stupendous achievement!'

Applause breaks out. Irwin checks his uniform, his suit should be cleaned and back in his room by now, but to hell with it – this is a good look, he loves it – guns and all! He steps forward into the room, it's the final breakfast and all the Americans are there. On seeing Irwin the clapping dies out and the room goes silent. Irwin takes a bow, accepting the applause as his own.

'Why thank you for that! Just want to say goodbye. I'm riding on outta here today with my new stock. Hope you all had a good trip. Didn't work out quite the way I planned, but there you go. I've got me the best damn mares in the Perche - and what good's a stallion without an equally good mare? So I wish you all a safe trip home.'

He looks to Carrie with a knowing glint in his eye. She smiles. 'Thank you Mr. Gurd.'

He walks over to her, 'No, I thank you Ma'am.' He kisses her hand 'And I thank you a whole lot, Mr. Dunham, sir... I surely do…'

He huffs, puffs and mumbles, 'Maybe we owe you an apology.'

'You owe me nothing sir, I lied to you…' Irwin takes in the various tables, 'Mr. Ellwood, I guess you saw through me too. Oh and Mr. Quinn…'

Quinn looks nervous, never sure what this crazy man will do next. It's a bait Irwin can't resist.

'Did you hear? Your stallion? Fine spirited animal - he got out last night.'

'He what?'

'Clean jumped out of his stall and do you know what he did? The cheek of the fellow - he got in and mated with some of my mares!'

Quinn jumps up and stands there speechless, aware that all eyes are on him. Irwin turns his attention back to Carrie, 'If I could borrow Charles for a moment Ma'am.'

'Of course, you have much to discuss I should imagine.'

'We do Ma'am, we sure do.'

He congratulates his compatriots on buying up every decent horse in the Perche, reminds Dunham that it's now three thousand and *six* horses, doffs his cap and leaves, followed by a compliant, if reluctant, Charles. Quinn is still standing trying to work out the implications of this final joke on the part of the country boy.

In Charles's room it is soon clear to Irwin that working his passage on the Normandie was a much easier way to cross the ocean. Before he can sail this time he will have to meet up with an agent in Le Havre and the American consul who will provide the documents that he will need for boarding and entry to America. Charles provides the letters of introduction. In addition there appears to be an endless amount of paperwork relating to the bank account he has set up in Irwin's name. Loan facilities have also been arranged. He stresses the extraordinary generosity of Mrs. Dunham who is underwriting all his outgoings until he gets back home, 'And much, much more…' he says cryptically. Irwin is aware of a disapproving note in the man's voice – like this was more than just a financial favour. Was he jealous? Was an emotional involvement breaking the banker's code? No time to dwell on it – there were so many papers still to sign… Then in addition there's the matter of getting the horses onto the train – which is already full. Irwin can see Charles becoming increasingly stressed and he himself has had enough of the whole complicated business. He tells the banker not to worry his little head anymore. There's over a week before the boat leaves - he'll take the horses – it's what he's done all his life, a string of six horses is nothing; he'll walk 'em there. All Charles needs to do now is give him the francs he needs and he'll go pay for the goods. The money is counted out, Irwin gives Charles a big hug, the man's stiffness suggesting he's never had the like in his life before and he leaves. There's no good-bye because they will see each other on the boat – on the Normandie where he will have a cabin…

He's panicking as he takes the battered valise and heads across the yard to the stable. The paperwork has taken far too long. He should be meeting the uncle right now and what if Gaston has learnt of the deal and tries to scupper it? He's given the stable lads a list of things that he needs for the journey and they do Blanche up like a packhorse while Irwin takes food from Sidonie, slipping her a wad of francs. He tells her to look after Jacqueline which she seems to understand, a tear coming to her eye. He's about to mount up when he hears a familiar shout, 'Country boy!!'

Quinn is storming across the yard, 'What have you done? Where's my horse? You gone too far this time! Think you can make a fool of me?' He grabs Irwin who shoves him off at the very moment Gaston comes riding into the yard at speed. He shouts at Irwin as he jumps from the cart. He's looking mad like he must have found out… about what? Jacqueline? The mares? He's coming right at him. Irwin grabs Quinn and holds him in front of himself like a shield, whispering into his ear, ' Ask him – he knows where your boy is…' Then to Gaston, 'This is the man! That horse should'a been yours! Vive la France!' Quinn is now confused, 'He's got my horse?'

'Ask him!'

Quinn does so, now angrily suspecting Gaston. In moments the two men are shouting at each other, neither understanding a word the other is saying, a re-igniting of their earlier dispute. Irwin stirs it up a little then steps out of the fray, as Fournier comes into the yard and asks what's going on? In the confusion Irwin quietly mounts his horse and rides out of the hotel yard for the last time.

The uncle is still waiting at the farm, the horses are bridled up ready. Younger brother Jean is there but there's no sign of Jacqueline. Irwin's heart sinks. To be back in this place, hours after being in heaven here... and she's not around... Gaston hasn't stopped the deal, so what – he's found out about him and Jacqueline? He asks where she is. He asks if she's alright. They tell him nothing, faces hardening like it's out of bounds to even mention her name. The money - they are only interested in the money. It's counted out, the uncle suspicious of the large denomination notes, Jean reassuring him they're genuine. Irwin checks out his animals then ropes them together as he's done a hundred times before. He asks which road he should take. He doesn't understand their instructions, but can pick out the relevant words. He repeats 'Alençon' to them and they nod. He must remember that... That's the road he needs to take. It's the conclusion of the most sombre deal he's ever made. He shakes their hands, tells Jean he has the best sister in the world, 'Jacqueline... très bon, très, bon, très bon!' And finally the lad nods and smiles. It's an awkward kind of agony, these people don't want to communicate, he can't communicate and there's nothing else he can say or do. 'So... I guess that's it - a promise is a promise... and you boy - she's given you her life. I hope to God you appreciate that.' In spite of the language barrier Irwin feels the lad understands. Irwin mounts up, looks around one last time – is she hiding there somewhere? He loiters. There's not a sign, he kicks Blanche on and the solemn procession heads slowly off up the track, into the tunnel of trees and out onto the open road.

*****

On the other side of the world it's the worst of many bad days on the Gurd farm. It's a scene being repeated across the land. There'd been drought the year before, just one of the reasons business had been bad; crops had failed, many sod-busting families had lost everything. Many had moved on, corporations were buying up land, leaving Abe with no one to buy his stock. It was a good time to be a bailiff and they'd already been to make the inventory of the few saleable items left on the farm. There's a dread now descends as the family watch someone approaching on the far side of the valley. They've been waiting for the moment. The only confusion is the driver is alone and he's in a buggy, not on a wagon… and he's wearing a suit – a suit means more bad news – has he come to take the land itself? It's a young, fresh-faced lad has the reins, and he drives in smiling, just to twist the knife. 'Mr Gurd?'

He jumps down and takes a letter from his leather case. Mary-Anne steps forward to take it. Abe stops her, he's still the man of the family. He opens it as the youngster says cheery 'hellos' to Jed, Luke and Martha. Abe reads what's written. He looks up and stares at the messenger. Mary-Anne takes the letter from him and reads. She looks to Abe who now has tears flowing down his cheeks. He mumbles to himself, 'He's alive, the boy's alive!' He looks to Jed, 'Your brother's coming home.' There are shrieks from Luke and Martha. He hushes them up, speaking through tears, 'And he's bringing horses!'

The young man has driven all the way from the bank in Abilene. They insist he has a drink with them before he heads back, though they apologise for the quality of the coffee. He tries to answer their many questions, to reassure them about the contents of the note, which they appear to mistrust. He explains that the bank had received a telegraph message underwriting the family's debt. They were therefore to be given longer to repay their loans. Every piece of good news brings a further stream of tears from Abe, releasing weeks of anguish. Mary-Anne is the only one who remains poker faced. Yet again her future is being put on hold. The young man sips his hot drink which bears no relation to any cup of coffee he's ever tasted. He smiles, happy to be the bringer of good news, wondering how people still live like this in this day and age.

FIFTEEN

Jacqueline tries to tug the rope that's round her wrist. She's desperate to sit down but it leaves her arm stretched up in the air and her hand numb. She leans against the oak pillar and looks up. Somewhere up in the blackness she knows the rope goes over the beam and when she'd first seen him throw it over she thought he was going to hang her. If the family hadn't stopped him, maybe he would have – he'd have seen her dead one way or another she's sure of it. It was a whipping like she'd never had. Her brother said later that she asked for it and maybe she did. There was a perverse pleasure in letting her cousin know that after all the years she'd denied him her body, fought him tooth and nail when he groped her, that she'd then given herself willingly to a foreigner. Telling him was her moment of triumph and maybe she wanted to die. Maybe that's the only way out for her now. She licks the blood from the wheal on her arm. She's so tired… but tomorrow's another day and one way or another he will never win. She'll never be his, not now, not after this.

The door to the barn creaks open. She can see from the silhouette that it's her uncle. Only when he's shut the door does he light the lamp. He comes forward and holds it to her bruised face. She turns away, asking how his son expects her to love him, after what he's done. The uncle has to steady himself, holding the pillar. He whispers, telling her how he wished she'd never met that American, all they'd brought was trouble – given the young people false hope. He starts to undo the rope, hands shaking, struggling with the knots in the darkness. She says nothing, wondering where this can be leading, knowing the risk involved, both of them frightened to speak out loud. When she's free he comes close and confides how much her father loved her and how he'd promised him that he would always look after her. He can't do that here, that much now is certain. She must go up to Dechanel, take the best horse and head for the Alençon road. She'll catch him, without doubt – he's trailing six horses. This is the best he can do, the rest is up to her. She hesitates, worrying for him and the farm if she leaves. He urges her to go, no time for talking. He pushes her towards the door and snuffs his lamp. She can't believe what's happening, she has to hug the man one last time, trying to reassure him that it will be okay; her brother will still have the farm, she swears he will - she'll write to whoever and make sure of it, make sure he looks after them all. Once in the yard they daren't speak. She creeps along the side of the buildings, looks back one last time, nothing moving, her uncle already absorbed by the shadows. She makes her way up to Dechanel.

She gives herself no time to think, she gropes around desperately in the barn, finds her father's old saddle, runs back to the field, takes the first horse that comes to the gate and is soon riding away as though her evil cousin was already in pursuit. She doesn't slow down until she passes the boundary of her known world. It's not that far but it's heading away from the town in an unfamiliar direction. She's on a road she doesn't know and she realises that she is about to travel further than she has ever been in her life. She can hear the girls in the convent whispering stories of life in the cities, making it sound like a great adventure, but it's daunting now – she has nothing! She's a woman riding alone and if she's on the wrong road, if she doesn't find Irwin what will she do? End up, like they did, in dark alleyways with faceless soldiers? One thing is certain – she can't go back. She spurs her horse on, but as soon as it's daylight she can see her dress is blood stained and she assumes her face is a similar mess. She has to find water. She goes off the road to a line of trees, knowing it will mean a stream. She strips off and washes herself and her dress, the cold water first stinging then soothing and numbing the unseen wounds on her back. She can't linger, she's panicked, wringing out her dress, putting it on wet and heading back to the road terrified of never catching up with her man. He had over half a day's march on her, but would he ride through the night like she had?

She can't know it but Irwin has stopped several times, partly to graze the horses, but also to reconsider. Not for the first time in his life, certainty has deserted him and he finds himself riding one way with a conviction that he should be going in the opposite direction. How can he leave her? But then how can he not go home? Carrie had told him that he will get over it, his love-sickness, everyone does, but right now that was impossible to believe. He's haunted by the raging face of Gaston in the hotel yard; the eyes of a wounded animal, he had come to kill him, he's sure of it, so what will he do to Jacqueline? She's all he can think about, it had kept him awake in the night as he tried to sleep on his blanket by the roadside. Now, he doesn't know it, but he's taken the horses to the very same stream in which Jacqueline had bathed, he's washed his face maybe in the same water, in her blood… if it could carry a message it would be saying *wait for me!* Not by chance he's doing just that, he's giving the mares more time to graze, he's walking around riddled with indecision, he decides he can't do it – he can't leave her! He knows the whole world will say he's crazy, nothing new there, and he knows how much of his future he's putting at risk, but he can't do it – he will not abandon her now. He mounts up, apologises to Blanche and turns her to lead them all back the way they had come.

It had been a cold, clear night and a mist was being slow to lift in the valley. The chill was also getting to the bones of both Jacqueline and Irwin; she with her damp dress clinging to her skin and he with a growing sense of foreboding. She is starting to shiver and lose heart when she first sees this mirage – a man heading towards her in the mist with a string of horses... She screams, kicks her horse on, desperate to make it real, terrified it will disappear, not quite believing… He hears a scream, shoots awake from bad thoughts, he too can't believe what's coming towards him. 'Go Blanche!' It's a moment before the whole string breaks into a trot. He can hear her clearly now, she's yelling his name, 'Irwin!!'

They meet and she collapses sobbing into his arms. He comforts her. 'It's alright, I was coming to get you, it's alright. Everything's going to be alright.' He feels guilty, seeing her bruised face, feels bad that he ever left her. He swears he'll never leave her again.

They ride off the road, he gives her his cavalry shirt, wraps her in a blanket, hangs her dress on a tree to dry. He manages to light a fire and they share a cigarette. They kiss and hold each other, letting the warmth return. It's a long time before they get to really speaking, what's happening feels too big for words, it's the whole of their lives that's changing here, changing forever. They share the bread and cheese Sidonie had prepared for him and then the questions begin, 'You do want me don't you?'

That's an easy one for Irwin, she's all he wants in the world. 'And you do want to go to America?'

'You promised.'

'Then that's settled then, when would I ever break a promise? I guess we gotta go catch us that boat.' And they hit the road together, riding side by side, every so often looking at each other and laughing, not quite believing their luck.

It's three days later when they finally reach Le Havre and another two days before the paperwork is sorted. It's not Irwin's finest hour. If you've bullshitted your way through life, facts written down in black and white can be your undoing. He has to get Jacqueline onto the boat so insists that she's his wife. They need proof and she needs papers. The bureaucracy seem to have defeated them until Jacqueline mentions the magic word 'Dunham.' She insists that she knows boys that have travelled before to look after his horses on the boat; that's all they're doing – they're accompanying the horses. This appears to tick the boxes the officials need, and eventually their passage is booked – they will be travelling with the horses. It's Jacqueline who ends up sorting out all the documentation for both them and the animals. Irwin is very impressed, it's not only because she speaks the language, it's the fact that she can be bothered, that she enjoys arguing with the most boring people in the world. She can make them turn a definitive 'Non!' into a gallic shrug and an official stamp. All he can do is keep telling her he loves her and he knows they're going to get along just fine!

Irwin is not so happy once they're on board. It's not the Normandie! It's a packet ship. He'd fantasised about a cabin with a flushing toilet. He'd promised Jacqueline… They're way down below deck, bunking in with stable lads and poor families hoping for a life in the New World. There are hundreds of horses meaning that Irwin is working his passage once again, literally mucking in and mucking out with the lads. Jacqueline doesn't mind at all, this is what she's dreamed of for years. Their task is to ensure that Blanche and their half dozen mares know they're with them, to keep them calm, however rough it gets, however much the other animals are panicking. She's happy staying with them but not when she feels the boat begin to move. When they leave port she's up on deck. It's the first time she has ever seen the sea and she can't drag herself away from the rail. Ever larger sails are raised, huge sails, the wind fills them and they are carried out onto the ocean. Irwin is equally in awe, he'd seen nothing of this on the Normandie. They watch as all trace of land disappears behind them, nothing but the sea now in every direction and that's when it really sinks in; no going back now. They cling together and stare into the great unknown.

SIXTEEN

Carrie Dunham gave birth to a third child ten months after leaving Normandy. This was a month after Jacqueline and a month before one of the mares gave birth to the first Norman horse on the Gurd farm. A second foal was delivered a week later and to everyone's delight, it was a very healthy colt.

Dunham had chastised his wife for what he described as reckless behaviour during their visit to Normandy. Arrangements she had entered into were the result of emotional weakness, letting her heart rule her head. She didn't see it like that at all. She was happy to admit that she adored Irwin, but where was the harm in that? She'd seen men behave far more recklessly when away from their wives, only to leave broken hearts behind. She was abandoning no-one. Irwin still had a very special place in her life. He was her protégé and she would continue to support him. This was how Irwin came to be the agent for Dunham and Co. in Bluff County. It was just as well, it would be years before his and Carrie's investment would pay off; before his horses would be winning awards in Chicago.

It was Carrie alone who allowed Irwin's dream to continue and Jacqueline who kept the dreamer's feet on the ground. The greatest thing about being in love was that it blinded her to the reality, first of the roughness of the crossing and then to the state of the Gurd farm. As long as she was with Irwin it was all a great adventure and she saw only possibilities in the impoverished little homestead that he brought her to. Of course it wasn't as he'd described, but she was used to that. She was used to poverty and knew how to make it work. That meant Irwin found himself working harder than he had since he'd laboured in the fire room of the Normandie. He had no time for fantasy. In addition to the horse business, they needed an extension to the cabin. They soon had geese and turkeys. There were cows and pigs picked up cheap from those moving West. There were fences to maintain, wells to be sunk. Jacqueline overcame Mary-Anne's initial hostility, the arrival of the baby brought the new life the place needed and above all the whole family was united by work, by the tasks that needed doing every hour of every day.

Carrie never went back to France. The enduring memory of one rough crossing with the children outweighed the romance. She was happy now to remain at home and let her husband go with his male associates. She had her own interests to pursue. This year, the baby is old enough to be left and while Mark is away she takes the train from Illinois to Kansas. Charles is with her, there are business matters that her husband, before he left, insisted needed attending to. Irwin meets them at the station in Abilene. He hopes his guests don't mind riding on an old wagon, 'The carriage is in for a polish…' Carrie smiles, pleased he hasn't changed. 'And you remember Blanche?' The horse's ears prick up on hearing her name. She hadn't taken kindly to the crossing, objected even more to pulling a buggy, but had come to realise it was the price you paid for running hell for leather across the plains. Carrie's amused by the large painted sign set above the driver's box; *Gurd and sons, the largest breeders and importers of Norman horses in Bluff County.* The silhouette of a black stallion below is very familiar and takes her straight back to the studio of Rosa Bonheur. *Agent for Dunham and co. of Wayne Illinois* is inscribed across the bottom in much smaller letters. She would let her husband know that he might be in smaller print than Irwin but his largesse wasn't being taken for granted.

She regrets not bringing the children, they'd been across oceans, seen the wonders of the Rocky mountains, but they should experience this – this is how their great grandparents had lived not so very long ago. She's enjoying every bump and shake of the wagon as Blanche hurtles across the grassland. Charles in the back is not so happy, clinging to the sides for fear of being thrown overboard.

The whole family are there to greet them when they draw up outside the cabin. Abe rises from his chair on the new veranda. Since Irwin's return a part of him has not dared to believe what he'd achieved, was waiting for it all to collapse – there had to be a catch!

But now as he watches his son helping this beautiful lady down from the buggy it all makes sense. Irwin suddenly looks like his own brother, Reuben. This is what he would have done if a bullet hadn't taken him. This is what he could have achieved. You have to be crazy! Abe doesn't move, he is happy to watch the whole scene unfold and he feels a weight lifting off his shoulders. This was more precious than any amount of gold. Irwin had referred to Carrie as an angel, and talked of his mother being with him all the way. He now knew what he was talking about and he somehow believed that she'd come home.

It was Jacqueline who had established a regular correspondence with Carrie. That's how their benefactor knew what was really going on and it was on that basis that she had advanced more funds, written off earlier loans. She eagerly awaited every letter; it was through Jacqueline that she could live a life that privilege denied her. It had brought the two women close and it was Jacqueline she was most anxious to see. She brought presents for the baby, they shared a bond and she realised the irony - if Irwin had taken her advice and turned his back on love, none of this would be happening. She had no complaints about her own life, how could she? But it did make her wonder as the young couple proudly show off the horses, as Irwin exaggerates how much the two young stallions would fetch in Chicago. There was something wonderful about being in at the beginning of a dream.

A table is set up outside the cabin and food and drink are brought out by the youngsters. As they take their seats Carrie is eager to know about every member of the family. Mary-Anne hovers around and approaches Charles with a face as dry as the cider she offers, 'You like a drink?'

She pours as Irwin grips his arm, 'Would you like a wife?'

Jacqueline cuffs the back of his head. Charles seems oblivious, 'I think my mother has that one under control, but thank you for asking.'

He continues, with no awareness of irony, to tell Irwin that Mr. Dunham was keen for him to understand that the value of his young stallions will be totally dependent on him ensuring that they are entered into the new Percheron stud book, 'The bloodline apparently is everything.'

Irwin chuckles and says a quiet thank you to Mr. Quinn. The memory of that night being one that he will treasure forever.

Jacqueline lifts little Sidonie onto her lap, explaining to her in French all about their guest. Carrie smiles, this place stirring her own memories. She looks around the neat little farm with the horses and other animals grazing and the home-made bread and cheese on the table… she's back in a little corner of France right there in Kansas.

****

Printed in Great Britain
by Amazon

67336025R00102